I0712836

lost in you

MINNESOTA MAMMOTHS
BOOK 1

BRENDA ROTHERT

Copyright © 2024 by Brenda Rothert

All rights reserved.

No part of this book may be reproduced in any form or by any electronic or mechanical means, including information storage and retrieval systems, without written permission from the author, except for the use of brief quotations in a book review.

Cover design by Kari March

TRINITY

"And influencer samples will be mailed by Friday?" Meeting with my team virtually via Zoom, I look up from my checklist. When I'm met by silence, I prompt, "Kelsie?"

"Yes." She smiles brightly. "Sorry, I just got the preprinted notecards that I'm putting in the boxes today and I paused when you asked because the order was short, but I can go to a print shop and get more made next week."

"Okay, what else?"

We're twenty-three days from the launch of Allura, the first drugstore line for Kiss My Sass, the cosmetics company I work for. And as a vice president of Allura's marketing department, I'm in charge of the team planning the launch. It wasn't a great time to take a couple of days away from the office to come see my older brother's pro hockey exhibition game in Fairbanks, Alaska, but here I am. Zooming from a gloomy hotel room.

As my team members detail the status of launch preparations, I glance between their faces on my laptop screen and the door to my hotel room. I know Ronan, the guy I went on two dates with a few months ago, isn't going to charge into the room because he doesn't have a key. Still, he figured out I was coming here and followed me. I'm panicking inside about what else he's capable of.

"Legal is still negotiating the Ella London deal," Jack says. "She wants more money."

"Dammit." His comment brings my mind back to the meeting. "What about all the videos we already had produced with her?"

"Hopefully we'll be able to use them. But legal says for now, we can't use her name, her likeness or any materials with her in them."

My heart pounds and I get the buzzing sensation in my head my anxiety always brings on. Ella London is an actress and model who's the backbone of Allura's marketing. Without her, we're screwed.

"When will this be resolved?" I ask Jack.

"I've tried to pin legal down, but—"

The sound of my hotel room door's lock clicking open makes my pulse pound nervously. It's not Ronan, but still...I can't stop fearing it might be until the door is pushed open and I see my brother Dalton walking inside.

And from his expression, I can tell he's pissed.

"Why aren't you at the police station like I told you?"

I glare at him. "I'm in the middle of a meeting."

In four seconds flat, he's already stomped all the way across my hotel room, where he looks at my computer screen and barks, "She'll call you back," before shutting it.

"Dalton! I'm their boss! That was so unprofessional." Dalton is a pro hockey player who intimidates people for a living, but I don't take shit like this from him.

He scowls down at me, hands on his hips. "Why the fuck am I just finding out some asshole is stalking you? How long has this been going on?"

I sigh heavily, the buzzing sensation returning.

"I went on two dates with him in October. He's been calling and texting since. He's shown up at my apartment a few times. But nothing like this has happened before."

I don't tell my brother that Ronan has probably been looking for me at my apartment a lot more than I'm aware of because I often sleep on the couch in my downtown Chicago office. The building security there is tight.

"So tell me what happened. Did he come up to you at the game, or did you just happen to see him?"

"I saw him walking toward me, waving like we knew each other. But the usher stopped him because I was in the VIP section. And then I told an usher what was going on and they had someone from security get me to a cab after the game so I could get back here."

My brother's eyes are blazing with fury. "I told you to go to the police station. What the hell were you thinking coming back here by yourself when some psycho is after you?"

My face is hot and I'm suddenly sweaty. Dalton is making this stressful situation even worse.

"I had a meeting." I reach for the bottle of

medication in my bag, my hands trembling as I open the bottle.

He looks up at the ceiling. "You had a meeting." When he looks at me again, he pinches the bridge of his nose. "You are the most incredible combination of smart and stupid I've ever known."

"I flew seven fucking hours to watch your game in a place where it gets dark before four p.m. Don't be an asshole. I have a launch in twenty-three days and that might not mean anything to you, but it means everything to me. I'm incredibly busy at work right now."

He puts a palm out. "You're right, I'm sorry. But Trin, this guy following you from Chicago to fucking Alaska has me on edge. If I could find him right now, I'd probably kill him."

He's always been overprotective. Partly because it's just who he is and partly because our dad died when Dalton was thirteen and I was ten. For the past sixteen years, Dalton has tried to be a big brother who fills as much of the space left behind by our dad's loss as he can, and I love him for that.

"I'll go to the police when I get home," I assure him. "And I'll--"

"You're not going home."

I pinch my brows together in a skeptical look.

"Yes, I am. My flight leaves at six twenty tomorrow morning."

"You're flying out of a small private airport as soon as I drop you off there. One of my teammates is going with you and he'll take you to my place in Minneapolis and stay with you until I get home."

My jaw drops. "No, absolutely not."

"I'd take you myself, but I have team captain shit tonight I can't miss. Interviews and stuff. Lincoln's my best friend on the team, I'd trust him with my life."

"It's not about you taking me or not taking me, I have to get home to prep for the launch."

He folds his arms across his chest and frowns. "You've told me you can work remotely."

My laugh is laced with the stress I'm feeling. "Not twenty-three days before a launch."

"You'll have to figure it out." He shrugs. "I'm not letting you go back home with this guy getting ballsier and ballsier about stalking you. I wouldn't be able to sleep at night."

I bury my face in my hands. "What if I told you it's not actually about you?"

"The fuck it's not. You're my sister."

"Dalton—" I give him an imploring look and he slices a hand through the air dismissively.

"You aren't moving in with me or anything, okay? This might only be for a day or two. Once the cops in Chicago find him and have a talk with him, you can go back home."

I stand, coming face to face with him, torn between aggravation and affection for my stubborn brother. "I can go home anytime I want because I'm a twenty-six-year-old adult."

He groans. "Just do this, Trin. Please. For me. I'm really worried about you." When I don't answer right away, he adds, "You know I'm right. It's not normal for a man to follow you to fucking Alaska when you went out with him a couple of times in October."

I exhale heavily, hating to admit he's right. The timing couldn't be worse, but Dalton is saying out loud what I've been denying for a while; I need to take Ronan's actions more seriously, whether it's convenient for me or not.

"Fine. But I can't stay more than a few days, and I mean that. I have to be in the office all week next week. I'm compromising now and I need you to be open to compromising too."

He considers. "I could always hire private security for you. We'll work it out."

I glance down at my watch. "When did you say we have to be at the airport?"

"There's a private plane and pilot on standby for us. Linc's meeting us there."

I pick up my cell phone from the desk. "Let me text my coworkers about my overbearing brother cutting off our meeting and then I'll pack my stuff."

"I'll pack for you." He starts toward my open suitcase on the king-size bed.

"No." I say it firmly. "You'll manhandle my stuff."

"Have you told Mom about your stalker?"

I scoff and look up from my phone screen. "What do you think? If I'd told her, you'd know about it."

"She's gonna flip her shit and fly straight to Chicago with her baseball bat."

His mention of our mom's "security system"—an old, solid wood baseball bat—when we were growing up makes me laugh. I don't doubt that Maria Lorenzo—all one hundred and twenty pounds of her--really could use that thing to take out someone who was threatening one of her children. I got my hazel eyes, strong work ethic and functional anxiety from her.

Well, mostly functional. If my mom flew in from

her Tampa retirement community because she was worried about the Ronan thing and stayed for more than two weeks, my anxiety would skyrocket. I love her more than anything, but the way she reorganizes my apartment and nags me about not dating makes me crazy after several days.

I text my work team, then quickly pack my belongings that are scattered around the room. Dalton shakes his head as he picks up my full suitcase.

"Did you really need all this for a two-night trip?"

"I didn't know how cold it would be."

He points at my boots, his brow furrowed. "I don't think you were worried about the cold when you bought those."

I glance at my suede Jimmy Choo ankle boots, purchased with a work bonus a few months ago. "These are lined with shearling. They're warm."

"You need tall, practical boots here. And a parka."

I slide into my cream-colored quilted coat. "I didn't ask you for fashion advice. And this was just a quick visit. I won't be coming back to Alaska in January ever again."

"You ready?"

I nod. "And congrats on the win, by the way."

"Thanks, but it was an exhibition, so it doesn't count." He opens the hotel room door, using his arm to hold me back while he looks up and down the hallway.

"Checking for snipers?" I crack.

"Laugh it up," he says with a glare. "I'm just trying to keep you from ending up stuffed in some psychopath's trunk."

My mom and brother can guilt me like no one else. "I know. I'm sorry."

He leads the way to a rental SUV, locking me inside the vehicle before taking his eyes off me so he can load my suitcase into the back. When he unlocks his door and gets in beside me, I smile, not letting on how stressed I am.

My boss, Gloria, would understand why I'm going to Minneapolis if I explained it to her. Her first husband was abusive and Gloria now serves on the board for an organization that supports survivors of domestic abuse. She'd probably pull me off the launch campaign and tell me to work on something else until I feel safe returning to Chicago.

That's the last thing I want. I've worked hard to get here. So many early mornings, late nights and quick lunches eaten at my desk. Everyone at the company knows the Allura launch is my baby. I even got to sit in on a meeting with Kate Ryker, our CEO. If I'm taken off the project now, others will get credit for my hard work, and there won't be another opportunity like this for a long time.

All because a fucking man couldn't take no for an answer. I'm completely over domineering alphas who expect every woman to fall to her knees over them.

I tell Dalton about the Allura launch on our drive to a small, private airport outside Fairbanks. He listens while checking the rearview mirror every minute or so to make sure nothing is amiss. If we encounter Ronan, I don't even want to think about what my brother might do to him.

When Dalton parks, gets out and closes his door, I open a bottle in my bag, take out a pill and swallow it. Hydroxyzine should help tamp my anxiety over flying in a small plane.

As soon as I step out of the vehicle in the airport parking lot, a blast of icy air smacks me in the face and throws open my unbuttoned coat. There are no trees and very few buildings here to block the wind, and the painful cold of it is a shock to my system.

I pull up my hood and button my coat, keeping

my head down as I follow Dalton. We walk into a building that's more like a large shed, nothing but two men standing by a desk littered with Styrofoam cups and overflowing with paper.

"Hey," one of the men says to Dalton as we approach. "This is our pilot, Chris Stanton."

Dalton shakes Chris's hand and glances over at me. "This is my sister Trinity. Trin, Lincoln and Chris."

Lincoln shakes my hand first, his expression so serious it's almost a frown. He's tall, with broad shoulders, dark hair and coffee-colored eyes. In his parka and knee-high boots, he looks more like a rugged local hunting guide than a hockey player.

As soon as our handshake ends, he looks at the door to the building and scans the sparse interior, seeming to verify we're still the only three people in here.

"Trinity, I'm Chris." Our pilot is the opposite of Lincoln. He looks around fifty, his silver hair cropped short. Beneath his coat, he's wearing a bright Hawaiian shirt and he's grinning. "You ready to take a little ride in Gertie?" He leans in slightly. "That's what I call my plane. She's my pride and joy."

"Sure." I force a smile. "Thanks for taking us on such short notice."

He shrugs and laughs. "Hey, you know what they say about money talking. She's all fueled up and waiting."

Dalton and Lincoln exchange a look and Dalton says, "The sooner you can get her out of here, the better."

"I'll take good care of her," Lincoln promises.

I suppress an eye roll. They're talking about me the same way Chris talks about his plane. Like I'm a thing instead of an adult who's *right here*.

Dalton passes Lincoln my suitcase. "I know you will, brother. Text me as soon as you land."

Lincoln nods and holds out a hand, indicating I should follow behind Chris. "I'll be right behind you."

I think these two are seriously overestimating Ronan, but I know Dalton is only trying to protect me, so I give my brother a quick hug and follow Chris.

It's just a quick plane ride and hopefully, a few days in Minneapolis. No big deal.

LINCOLN

Trinity seems to be a nervous flier.

She's grabbing the armrests on her seat so hard there are indentations beneath each of her fingers —and we haven't even taken off yet.

"I'm not just your pilot, I'm also your flight attendant," Chris says with a grin, turning his head around to look at us from his seat. "Sorry I'm not a cute redhead. I need your seat belts on for the entire flight. We'll be making a quick refueling stop in Atlin, but we won't be able to depart the plane. In the unlikely event of a water landing, there's a life raft hanging up there." I glance to the spot he's pointing at near the back of the tiny six-seater plane. "Parachutes next to the raft, first aid and survival kits. If you're gonna puke, no shame in that, but please use the bucket." He gestures at a small plastic pail affixed to the wall.

I almost took him up on his offer to sit next to him up front so I could enjoy the view, but I figured I should sit next to Trinity. She's not much for conversation, though. Every question I ask is answered with one or two syllables.

Chris starts the plane and begins communicating with air traffic control through his headphones. Trinity and I both have headphones on, too. It's the only way we can hear Chris over the noise of the plane.

Which is fucking tiny. I'm crammed into my seat, which is one of only six, including the pilot's. I'm used to traveling on the Mammoths' team plane, where I can recline my seat and stretch my legs out. My knees are currently pressed into the seat in front of me and my hands are in my lap, my shoulders squeezed together awkwardly so I can give Trinity the entire armrest area between us.

This is for Dalton, though. He's like a brother to me. I didn't hesitate when he asked me to leave the road trip early and get his sister back to Minneapolis safely.

Once Chris finishes all his preflight communications, he flips a few switches and looks over his shoulder at us. "Hold on to your hats, folks. It's windy today. Gonna be a rocky first leg."

Trinity cringes.

"Gertie'll get you there, don't worry!" Chris assures her. "If the bucket starts to get too full, let me know and I'll get out a trash bag."

Awesome. Who exactly will be flying the plane while he digs out a trash bag, I wonder?

The plane lurches slightly as it starts to move. Trinity presses her head back against her seat, holding her breath and squeezing her eyes shut.

"Hey, breathe," I remind her, patting her hand.

She ignores me, her face getting red. We aren't even off the ground yet and I'm worried she's going to pass out.

"Trinity, breathe." My tone is stern this time.

"I'm breathing; leave me alone," she snaps.

The color starts to return to her face because she had to breathe to respond to me. This is going to be a long flight.

I take in the view from the window beside me as we ascend, the landscape a sea of sparkling snow.

Minnesota winters are cold as shit, and it snows nonstop, but January in Alaska seems to be relentless. I've only been here for a couple of days and it's snowed more often than not. The temperatures are punishing, and it doesn't help that the sun only shines about six hours a day.

The team outfitted all of us with parkas, extra thick socks and knee-high all-weather boots for this trip. Or I should say, a sponsor did. We wore a little patch on our uniforms with the company logo.

As the plane climbs higher, it starts to pitch from side to side and lurch lower for a few seconds at a time. When I glance over at Trinity, her elbows are on her knees and her face is in her hands.

"This is all totally normal, right?" I ask Chris over the headset, hoping to reassure her.

"Oh yeah. Bush planes aren't made to ride as smooth as commercial ones, but Gertie's a workhorse. She'll get us there."

Within a couple of minutes, Trinity's face is hovering over the bucket. Poor kid. Dalton said she's twenty-six years old—eight years younger than me—but seeing her like this makes her seem younger.

"Just do it," I tell her. "You'll feel better."

She looks over at me, scowling. "Believe me, if I could, I would."

I see so damn much of Dalton in her. I'm the team captain and two years older than him. I've had to talk to him about his shitty attitude a few times. His intense competitiveness can give him tunnel vision, and as his teammate, I get it. But he's short-tempered at his best and a total asshole at his worst when he's under pressure, and some of our front office people find him abrasive. Reporters aren't big fans, either.

"You're a lot like your brother, you know that?" I ask Trinity, hoping to distract her from her misery.

She sits up, narrowing her eyes. "What's that supposed to mean?"

"Friendly." There's a note of sarcasm in my tone.

She scoffs. "Oh, for fuck's sake. *You're* the one who's like my brother. Expecting all women to fall at your feet because you're a big, strong hockey player."

I shrug, amused by her irritation. "Unfortunately there's no room at my feet right now."

She rolls her eyes. "That is unfortunate. You

know, there's a--" She tops talking and leans over the bucket, puking into it.

She does it over and over until she's dry heaving. The plane drops so hard and fast that she screams and I brace my hands against the seat in front of me.

"It's just a little snowstorm," Chris says through the headset. "Shit." He rubs his shoulder like it's bothering him. "Get the lid on the puke bucket, or we'll all end up covered in it."

Trinity flips the lid closed on the bucket and snaps a latch to lock it. She looks over at me, the fight gone from her expression. "I don't know if I can do this all the way to Mi--"

She stops when the plane plummets again, this time shifting from side to side, too. My stomach rolls with nausea, which has never happened to me on a plane.

My pride won't let me admit this turbulence is unnerving to me, too. My head bounces off the back of the headrest, the contact so rough it makes my teeth rattle.

Trinity is crying. I cover her hand with mine.

"We're gonna be okay," I promise. "Take some slow, deep breaths."

"I have to get off of this plane," she says weakly.

"Please."

I don't disagree. I'm thinking I can rent a car in Atlin and drive us the rest of the way.

The plane does another stomach-rolling drop and I lean forward, putting a palm on Chris's shoulder. "Hey man, how much longer until we get to Atlin?"

He doesn't respond. I unfasten my seat belt and lean forward, my heart pounding so hard I can feel the rush of it in my ears.

Chris's chin is on his chest and his eyes are closed. I grab his shoulder and shake him, but he doesn't move.

This is bad. Really fucking bad.

"Chris?" I put my hand on his neck, checking for a pulse. Though I don't feel anything, I'm not sure I'm checking in the right spot.

"Lincoln, what's going on?" Trinity practically wails. "Chris? Chris, what's happening?"

I get a good look out the plane's windshield and my jaw drops. The view that was a bright-blue sky is now a dense forest spotted with white snowcaps.

We're not far from the ground. I do the math quickly. Even if I could fly this thing—which I can't—I don't have time to get Chris out of his seat and take over the controls before we hit the ground.

"Holy shit!" Trinity screams. "We're going to crash!"

All we can do is brace for impact. I sit down, quickly get my seat belt back on and look over at Trinity. The plane drops farther and she screams again.

I close my eyes for a couple of seconds. This is going to be it. There were things in my life I should have made right but never did. I told myself I'd do it someday. Remorse and shame wash over me as I picture my dad.

"We have to get out!" Trinity unfastens her seat belt and starts to get up. "The parachutes!"

I don't stop to think. I just throw my arms around her waist and pull her against me.

"No, don't!" She tries to fight, but it's useless.

I force myself to breathe. I'm on the cusp of clinching a Mammoths team record for most goals scored, and now I'll never do it. I'm going to die in a plane crash six goals short.

We're nose-diving hard now. My heart feels like it's going to stop just from the horror of anticipation.

"Lincoln!" Trinity struggles to break free, but it's no use.

"We don't know how to use the parachutes."

I'm holding her as tightly as my arms will allow. "And we don't know how to fly a plane. We're going to brace ourselves and--"

"Die," she whimpers. "We're going to die."

A shiver races through me as I hear and feel the bottom of the plane scraping on treetops. Trinity presses her face against my chest and I lay my cheek on her hair. It's soft and smells like fresh rain. At least the last thing I'll ever smell in this world is her hair. There are far worse things.

The nose of the plane makes contact all at once, my arms locked around Trinity as my upper body rockets forward. It's like a bone-rattling body check into the boards during a game.

The roar of the engine goes silent and all I hear is a beeping sound. Trinity's heart races against my chest. A couple of seconds tick by as we both breathe; neither of us seems to believe it.

"We're alive," she cries softly. "Oh my God, we're still alive."

I release my hold on her slightly and our eyes lock for a second. I exhale heavily, then suck in a deep breath, still reeling. Then I lower my brows, sniffing.

"Do you smell that?"

Her eyes widen. "Smoke."

three

TRINITY

"MY BAG!"

I can't make sense of anything. The nose-down position of the plane means we have to climb up to get out of the plane, and the smoke is making it hard to see. My medication is in my bag, but it's not within reach.

"Fuck your bag, get over here!" Lincoln barks.

He's reaching through the smoke for me, and I take his hand. He pulls me over my seat and we climb over the next row. I'm dizzy, either from the crash or my own anxiety. I try to steady myself by putting a hand on the plane's wall and taking a deep breath. The smoke I'm inhaling makes me cough and feel even worse.

"We're getting the fuck off this plane," Lincoln says fiercely.

I crouch on the back of a seat as he turns the handle to the nearest door and tries to open it. He's working against gravity, and it doesn't budge. He takes a step back and throws his weight behind it, ramming his shoulder into it. The door moves a few inches before slamming closed again.

"There's something blocking it," he mutters.

It's getting harder to breathe. Silent tears stream down my cheeks and drip off. I'm just a few seconds away from getting hysterical. Did we just survive a plane crash only to die of smoke inhalation?

"Emergency exit in the back." Lincoln gets there quickly in the small plane, my heart in my throat as he turns the handle and pushes.

The door opens. I let out a sob as he reaches down for me. There's nothing for me to hold on to, so he has to pull me up on his own. He practically shoves me out the door, which is fine by me. Anything to get out of the plane.

I suck in a big gulp of fresh, freezing air as I climb out, holding on to the door opening. Now I can see that we crashed in a forest, the plane landing in a massive pine tree. There's nothing but open air around me.

"Get to the ground!" Lincoln orders. "This thing could blow at any second!"

No time to worry about the potential pitfalls—I jump. My arms instinctively fly up to protect my face from the scrape of branches on the way down. It's only a few seconds before I hit the hard ground on one foot, then land on my hip. Everything hurts.

It takes me a few seconds to be able to inhale fully, but I'm alive. I roll onto my back, horrified by the flames I see through the opening where the plane's windshield used to be.

Something that looks like a dark blur flies out of the airplane's exit door, followed by something red.

I get to my knees, planning to stand up, but as soon as I try to bear weight on my left ankle, pain shoots through it and I drop back to my knees. That's the one I landed on.

My bare hands can't handle being on the scattering of snow on the ground for long, so I kneel upright, pain shooting through my hip. I see movement in the tree the plane is lodged in—it's Lincoln, dropping from one branch to another.

He lands on the ground with both feet, then

stands upright. The moment his gaze lands on me I hate that I'll have to admit I jumped.

"You need help getting up?" He comes over to me, a hand extended.

"I hurt my left ankle." There. I didn't lie.

"Here, I've got you."

He puts an arm around me, supporting me so I can hop. I cry out with every movement, my entire body sore.

"I'm gonna get you to a safe distance and then I need to run back for the survival and first aid kits."

"That's what you threw out of...ow...the plane."

"Yeah, and there was a moving pad too. Figured we could use it."

Use it. Because we're stranded in Alaska and it's bitterly cold.

"What about Chris?" I lock eyes with him and his shoulders drop.

"If he wasn't already dead before we crashed, he is now."

I know he's right, but it's still horrifying. Chris was just alive, and now he's gone. Lincoln and I were lucky to live through the crash, but we're in the middle of nowhere.

"Someone will know where we crashed." I say the words out loud, though they're meant to reassure me more than anything. "Chris put in a flight plan and they'll know where we went off course."

An image of our smiling pilot in his Hawaiian shirt makes my heart sink. I'm still too stunned to really feel any of this yet.

"Right." Lincoln glances down at me. "Sorry about this."

"Wh--"

He bends and sweeps me into his arms, my breath whooshing out as my feet leave the ground. My ankle bounces as he jogs and it feels like someone's pounding on it with a sledgehammer.

"Put me down! Dammit, that hurts! I jumped out of the plane and I might have a broken ankle."

He gently deposits me on the ground, giving me a puzzled look. "You jumped out of the plane?"

Before I can respond, he stands up and turns around. "I have to get the stuff. Don't move."

I shake my head because I couldn't move if I wanted to. I close my eyes, reminding myself we're going to be rescued. I don't have any medication to calm my anxiety right now, but my therapist would tell me this anxiety is okay. This is my body's natural response to what's happening to me.

A minute later, Lincoln returns and drops the

supplies on the ground. He gets down on one knee and looks me over. "Where are you hurt?"

I groan and mutter, "Everywhere."

He creases his brow. "Is anything bleeding?"

"I don't think so."

"Lift your arms."

I do, and he pats down my arms and sides, then does the same to my legs. "What hurts the most?"

"My ankle and my hip. That's where I hit the ground."

"Can I take a look?"

I balk at his suggestion. "It's bitterly cold; I'm not taking my clothes and boots off. Help will be here within a few hours, we just need to stay near the plane and keep warm until then."

A flare of aggravation passes over his face. "It's going to be dark soon, and they probably don't know exactly where we crashed. We need to plan for the worst."

I scoff. "Then we should probably start digging a couple of graves."

My dark joke doesn't hit. He glares at me. "I'm doing everything I can to help you, don't give me a shitty attitude."

I hold my arms out to gesture at our

surroundings. "Our plane just crashed in…are we still in Alaska?"

"Yes," he snaps.

"Alaska in January. It's fucking freezing, we have no food or water and I can't walk."

"You can't walk because you *jumped out of the plane.*"

"You said to get out! That it could blow at any second!"

"That doesn't mean jump and blow out your ankle."

I scowl at him. "Well, this is my first plane crash. I didn't know what to do."

He sighs heavily and closes his eyes. "We're not gonna fight. I'm sorry. It's really important that we keep our cool and help each other through this."

His apology deflates my anger. "I'm sorry, too. I know it was dumb of me to jump."

"No, it wasn't. I was yelling at you to get out. We're not bringing up that subject again. It's done. What matters is that neither of us is bleeding out. We'll be okay until help arrives."

I nod, rubbing my hands together. Now that the shock is wearing off, I'm really feeling the icy temperature.

Lincoln grabs the survival kit. "Let's see if there's anything in here we can use."

"Maybe a flint to start a fire."

He sets the case between us and we both scan the contents. It has a flint, three water purification straws, flares, emergency blankets, a flashlight, a knife, nonperishable food, rubbing alcohol and a few other small things.

Just looking at it makes my heart race. I check myself. We won't need most of it. The flint will help us make a fire to keep warm and the flares will allow us to signal help when it's close. We're surrounded by snow, so we can't run out of water. Everything will be fine.

"Do you know how to use a flint?" I ask Lincoln, grabbing it.

He meets my eyes, his expression grim. "I grew up in an apartment in Columbus. I don't know shit about the outdoors."

"That's okay. I used to hunt and fish with my dad before he died. I know enough to get us by. We'll need some dry wood. Look deep inside some of the bigger pine trees for dried branches we can use to get the fire going."

He meets my gaze and nods. There's a crashing sound in the direction of the plane, like a part of it falling to the ground, and I tamp down the rise of panic inside me.

We're going to be okay. Help is on the way.

EIGHT HOURS LATER, I'M FREEZING DESPITE ALL efforts to warm up. We have a fire going and Lincoln insisted I wear his parka. I have the hood tied so it covers as much of my face as possible, and I have an emergency blanket on my legs, but the cold is soaking into me from the ground.

Lincoln is wrapped in the emergency blanket, my pink-plaid cashmere scarf wrapped around his head and ears. We're both huddled by the fire. He's sitting and I'm curled up on my side.

There's a howling in the distance, but this time, I don't even flinch. The first few times, I turned my back to the fire, watching to see if anything would try to approach us, but now I'm just too tired.

My ankle is so swollen it's painful to have my boot on, but I can't take it off due to the cold. The rest of me aches slightly less since I took some ibuprofen from the first aid kit.

If I can slip off to sleep, maybe I'll wake up to help arriving. No more worrying and enduring the icy temperatures. Lincoln doesn't look like he'll be able to sleep, so he'll let me know if any animals approach.

It's been so many hours since we crashed that help has to be coming any minute now. Surely this ordeal is almost over.

four

LINCOLN

IT's DARK, BUT THE FLICKERING FIRE CASTS ENOUGH light for me to see Trinity staring me down. I raise my voice this time, trying to get through to the stubborn-as-shit woman I've been freezing my ass off with for the past sixteen hours.

"Put the goddamn boots on. I don't have the energy to keep arguing with you."

"No." She stretches the word into three syllables this time like I'm too dense to comprehend it. "Then you won't have any boots and you'll get frostbite."

"You might already have frostbite in those

ridiculous boots of yours. Put the fucking boots on, Trinity."

It's late morning here, but it's still dark. Trinity slept for a few hours, but I only dozed off for about ten minutes while sitting up. I've been pacing to try to generate body heat, but when Trinity told me a few minutes ago that she couldn't feel her toes, I took my boots off and offered them to her. We've been engaged in a standoff ever since.

"We can't stay here," she says, catching me off guard.

"Yeah, that's the plan, but for now, you need to put these boots on."

She shakes her head, her expression mournful as she looks up at me from the ground.

I bend down so we're at eye level and give her my most menacing glare. "I don't want to wrestle you to the ground and put them on you, but I will if I have to."

She holds my gaze, completely unfazed. "No, you won't. Without those boots, you have nothing for your feet. At least I have something, even if these aren't the greatest."

A growl rumbles in my chest. "Those aren't enough for you if you can't feel your toes."

"We need to find shelter."

"We can build one here. We have to stay near the plane. Otherwise there's no way we'll be found."

She stands up, whimpering as she tries to bear weight on her left foot. Snowflakes are floating downward, dampening the fire so much I can barely make out the outline of her now.

"It's too cold and wet," she argues. "We can see if it's safe to get back in the plane if you want to, but I don't know if we'll be able to have a fire there."

I look at the ground. "No, I already checked it. There's not much left and it could fall out of the tree any second."

A few moments of silence pass before she continues. "Trained rescuers will be able to track us. It's not that I want to go, but we have to. It's too cold here. We have one good coat and one good pair of boots between us."

"There's no place to go," I remind her. "The view out the plane windows was just trees and snow. And you can't walk."

It wasn't just the cold that kept me up all night, staring forlornly into the fire. The seriousness of our situation settles deeper into my bones with every passing hour. I'm still hoping for rescue, but I can't help my mind wandering to what will happen if they can't find us.

I hear her sigh softly. "I know. But you know I'm right."

She sniffles, probably an indication she's crying. Fuck. I'm a leader, but I'm used to leading a bunch of male hockey players. I generally tell them to nut up. And we're never in life-or-death situations.

It's bitterly cold here, even though we're sheltered from some of the wind. Trinity is right about the coat and boots situation, and the moving pad and emergency blankets just aren't enough, either. My mind and body have slowed down a lot, and I've been telling myself it was just the lack of sleep and cold, but deep down, I know Trinity is right. Our survival plan can't just be hoping help will arrive any minute.

The weight of my promise to Dalton sits heavily on my shoulders. What if we leave and then die looking for shelter? It feels like a lose-lose situation.

"We have to try," Trinity says, her tone a mixture of fear and determination.

"Give me a little bit to think about it."

"It's not just up to you."

I exhale heavily, wishing for just an hour of sleep. Just one hour to get my mind clearer.

"Promise me you won't leave without me. No matter what, we have to stay together."

"I agree. But I won't stay here and freeze to death just because you have a penis and I don't."

I snap at her, my patience eradicated by lack of food and sleep. "Fuck your feminism. We might freeze to death out there, too. I said I'll think about it. Now we both need to eat something and try to get some blood moving."

"I'll eat something if you put your boots back on."

I sit down and grab one of my boots, wishing I had the energy for a run to cool my frustration. "Eat or don't eat, it's up to you. I'm not playing your fucking games."

"Because not wanting you to lose your feet to frostbite is a game to me." She rolls her eyes.

I silently get both of my boots on, thinking about Dalton. He knows by now that we didn't arrive in Minneapolis, and I'm sure he's going crazy. My energy has to be spent taking care of his sister, not arguing with her.

At least we have the survival kit. I open it and take out two protein bars, passing one to Trinity. She takes it, still glowering at me.

The bar tastes like cardboard, but I still savor

every crumb. I'm running through scenarios in my head, not liking any of them.

And making an already bad situation even worse, now my feet are wet. I can't risk taking my boots and socks off to try to dry them and my feet over the fire because of the cold.

"Would we hear a plane if it was flying overhead?" Trinity seems to be over her mood. "Would they even look in the dark?"

"I don't know if we'd hear it. I think they'd look, yeah."

"Do you think we should be out in the open where we can see a plane if it flies overhead so we can shoot the flare gun?"

I scrub a hand down my face. "That makes sense, yeah. But it's a lot colder out in the open."

"Yeah."

A few seconds of silence pass before I ask, "How are you feeling?"

She shrugs. "Worn down."

"Are you sore?"

"Yes, but I don't want to use any more of the medicine; we might need it later." She smiles ruefully. "If bears bite our legs off, Tylenol can help with the pain, right?"

I exhale a single note of laughter. "Chris

should've put a bottle of whiskey in that survival kit."

Her expression turns serious. "If we're going to look for shelter, we need to travel when there's light."

That'll only last for around six hours. This is a decision we're making together, but no matter what, I'm responsible for what happens to us. If anything happens to Trinity, it'll be on me.

"Fucking Alaska. Our exhibition game was in Florida last year."

She stands up, wincing as she brushes snow and dirt from her pants. "Eating that energy bar helped."

"No offense, but I don't think walking through the snow with a busted ankle will be any easier because you ate an energy bar."

"I'd take an Uber if I could, but my phone was on the plane." Her tone is light.

I reach into my pocket and take my phone out. "I've got mine, but it's useless. No service."

My pile of firewood has dwindled to almost nothing. I throw the last decent-sized log on the fire and say, "I need to go get more wood."

"Lincoln. We can't stay here."

"We're staying until the sun comes up. We need

to get as warm as we can before we set off to find the nearest Hilton."

She scoffs. "We might find a cave where we can get dry. Out of the wind."

Or we might find nothing but miles of snow. I don't say it because we both know it already. The thought of rescuers telling Dalton they found our frozen bodies in the middle of nowhere makes my chest ache.

"We'll try," I say cautiously. "But if it's nothing but snow and wind, we might have to come back here."

Even though it's too dark for our eyes to meet, I can feel her looking at me across the fire. "If anything happens to me, tell my m--"

I cut her off. "No. There's nothing to tell anyone because you're going to be fine. This will end up being your best story at parties someday."

"I hope so." There's a sad smile in her voice.

"Look, I know I haven't been all that encouraging, but we have to stay positive. Help is on the way. We just need to be smart and stay hydrated and warm while we wait."

"Right."

"The survival kit has a pad of paper and pencil. I'm going to leave a note at the plane."

Her voice is stronger as she says, "I'll come with you."

I wrap an arm around her to support her as she walks, only limping a little. Her boots are fucking ridiculous—probably some designer shit.

Can't say I'm surprised. Dalton told me she works in the cosmetics industry. I'll do whatever I have to do to get us both through this and then I'll have a good party story, too. The time I survived a plane crash with Wilderness Barbie.

five

TRINITY

THIS WAS A BAD IDEA. WE'RE JUST GOING TO FREEZE to death faster out here in the open, where the wind blows snow directly into our faces.

I've thought about how awful it would be to die by drowning or fire. Ironically, I've also considered how horrible going down in a plane crash would be, knowing you were plunging to your death for however long it took to hit the ground. Even with my propensity for worrying about things that probably won't happen, I've never wondered what it would be like to freeze to death.

Until now.

We set out from the wooded area many hours ago and we haven't seen any sign of shelter. Sometimes we pass through groupings of trees where we get a break from the wind, but mostly we've just been walking through snow. It's about a foot deep in some places and up to my knees in others, thanks to drifting.

"Whose turn is it?" Lincoln turns around and looks at me. "Am I up?"

"Yeah, it's you. Fourth grade."

He told me when we set out from the forest that we needed to keep our minds occupied every minute because it would help us keep moving forward. We talked about our jobs and homes and I told him everything there is to know about my cat, Karma. Then I thought of this little exercise, where we each tell the other person everything we can remember about every year we went to school. We've already been through kindergarten (when I peed my pants and had to miss the class holiday party to go home and change clothes), first grade (when Lincoln broke his arm falling out of a tree), second grade (fairly uneventful for both of us), and third grade (Lincoln kissed his first girl and I won the spelling bee).

Everything hurts. It's not just my ankle but my

entire body. And cold isn't enough of a word for what it's like to be out here. It's a bone-deep pain that almost burns. The only way I'm able to keep putting one foot in front of the other is that I know I'll die if I stop.

"I had Mr. McGill for a teacher," Lincoln says, yelling so I can hear him over the wind. "He brought his golden retriever to school with him every day; her name was Cookie."

I want to stop walking. Scream. Cry. Quit. I'm exhausted. My chest hurts when I breathe. It's only thoughts of my mom and Dalton that keep me moving forward. My mom loves her two children with her whole heart, and it would devastate her to lose one of us, especially like this.

And Dalton will never forgive himself if we die. He put us on that plane, and even though the crash is in no way his fault, I know him and he won't feel that way. He'll spend the rest of his life eaten up by guilt over it.

"Tell me about Cookie," I yell at Lincoln's back.

I'm trying to step where he steps, even though my feet are soaked and half-numb. It takes less energy to step in an existing footprint than it does to make my own. Lincoln has a big stride, though.

"Cookie was the best girl. She played ball with

us at recess. She usually chilled in a dog bed next to Mr. McGill's desk, but sometimes she'd walk up and down the rows of desks and we'd all pet her."

"Did you work on your kissing technique in fourth grade?"

"Yeah, but not with Cookie."

My lips crack painfully when I smile. I don't know how either of us can still make lighthearted comments when we're probably marching to our final resting places, but Lincoln keeps saying we have to keep our minds from wandering to the worst-case scenario. I'm trying.

"We took a field trip to the children's museum in Cincinnati and that was my first time holding hands with a girl."

"Who initiated the hand-holding?"

He glances over his shoulder at me. "Me, of course."

"Right. Back when you were just a cave*boy*? Not yet a full caveman?"

He laughs. "All women like men to make the first move."

"Gay ones don't."

Another laugh. "True. But Amy Ackerman liked it when I held her hand. She wrote in my yearbook that I was the cutest boy in the whole school."

"Do you know what became of her?"

"Amy? Let's see…I think we went to school together until seventh grade and then her parents put her in a Catholic school."

Lincoln is wrapped in the moving pad and the metallic silver emergency blanket, my scarf still the only covering on his face and ears. I keep my focus on his back, telling myself that if he can do this without a coat and hat, I can do it while bundled in his parka.

Every step is so hard, though. My feet seem to be made of lead. Deep down, I know being in this kind of cold with wet feet isn't survivable for long. We'll both get frostbite.

I'd normally find the prospect of my feet slowly turning black and dying something worth getting upset about. I just don't have it in me, though. It's getting dark, and our gamble didn't pay off.

I'm vaguely aware I'm not moving anymore. My whole body still hurts. Instinct makes me curl up into the fetal position.

"Trinity!" Lincoln runs back to me, dropping his blankets and the survival kit and using both hands to lift me up. "What happened?"

"I can't." Emotion wells in my throat. "Take the coat and leave me."

"No fucking way," he says fiercely. "Get up."

"I'm so tired."

"We'll find something soon. I'm tired, too, but I'll carry you if I have to."

"No. It's my fault."

I don't have the energy to explain what I mean—it was my idea to set out like this. Without the right supplies. To leave the plane.

Lincoln grabs the parka, a hand on each side, and hauls me into a standing position. I stumble against his chest and he supports my hips, fresh pain shooting through my injured ankle.

"You're either walking, or I'm carrying you." His breath against my face is the only warmth I've felt in...who even knows anymore? "We either live together or die together, you hear me? I'm not leaving you." He digs through the survival kit and takes out another energy bar. "Eat this and let's fucking go. I know you're tougher than this."

His harsh tone awakens something inside me. I grab the energy bar and shake it at him. "Is this going to heal my ankle? Will it make my feet dry? This is just a slow death and you know it."

"Quit bitching. We've gotta work with what we have."

He rewraps himself in the blankets and I rip open the protein bar, breaking it in half. Even without a coat, he's still going and not complaining. I don't know why I resent his determination.

I pass him half the bar and he shakes his head. "You eat it; you need it more than me."

"Eat it and I'll keep walking."

He shakes his head and takes half of it, glaring at me as we both eat.

"I've got a lot more fourth-grade shit to tell you," he says when he's finished. "You gonna listen?"

"Can't wait." My tone is heavy with sarcasm and a smile plays on his lips.

He starts walking forward again and I drag my feet into motion. Would I really have just stayed back there and died if he'd let me? Am I really that weak?

"I had my first official girlfriend in fourth grade," Lincoln yells from in front of me. "Macy Rivera. And that was when I started travel hockey. I wanted to be a goalie but my coaches rotated all of us on all the positions."

I imagine a little Lincoln with his dark hair and

confident smile. Was he a born leader, or did he grow into the role? I don't have the strength it would take to ask him.

As he tells me all about his first year of travel hockey, I focus on breathing and walking. Deep breaths, in and out, while keeping pace with him. It doesn't feel like I can do this, but I'm doing it anyway. Instead of thinking about the cold and our dismal survival odds, I think about breathing and stepping in the footprints he leaves in the snow.

Just. Keep. Going.

It's almost fully dark now. We're stopping about every hour to eat snow so we don't dehydrate. We've made it through school recaps up to sixth grade, and my dark sense of humor is encouraging me to at least live until I can tell Lincoln about winning the school science fair in eighth grade with the hypoallergenic lotion I invented.

Will I tell him I nearly died in ninth grade? I normally don't talk about it, but I'm entirely out of fucks to give at this point. Lincoln was twenty feet away when I peed in the snow behind a pine tree an hour ago. We've known each other for less than forty-eight hours and he's already seen me at my worst.

I can hardly feel my feet and my ankle is

throbbing with pain. I just want to rest for a few seconds.

The second I stop walking, he somehow knows and turns around.

"No stopping," he barks. "No quitting."

"My ankle." I'm so weak the words are barely audible.

My body sways, the effort to keep myself upright almost too much. If I fall right now, there's no way I could get back up.

Lincoln growls at me, getting in my face. "Don't be a pussy."

"You don't know." Emotion wells in my throat.

"Am I carrying you?" he snaps. "It's either walk or be carried."

"You're an asshole."

"I'm the asshole who's keeping you alive."

"Fuck you!" I snarl back at him. "I'm the one walking on a busted ankle. I'm the one whose feet are probably frostbitten."

"Cry me a fucking river. Just walk while you do it."

I ball my hands at my sides, still icy even though I have gloves on, and scream "Fuck you" as loud as I can. The effort hurts my chest and my back, but there's a tiny bit of a spark in me now.

Lincoln walks back a few steps, still facing me. "Catch me and you can have a free kick to my balls."

"With a broken ankle? Thanks, asshole." Glowering, I advance toward him. He turns and keeps walking.

Catching him isn't an option. It's all I can do to breathe and move. I had a moment of weakness back there, but I'm myself again. I'm not giving up. If I don't make it, I'll fall face-first into the snow while walking.

I close my eyes for a brief second, silently asking my mom and Dalton to send me the strength I need to get back to them.

six

LINCOLN

Where the fuck is the rescue party? I'm trudging through snow that's higher than my knees, icy wind whipping my blankets around. When I glance over my shoulder to make sure Trinity's still there, she raises a gloved hand in the air, probably flipping me off.

I have to keep her moving and pissing her off is the most effective way of doing that. Do I really think she's a pussy? No, but calling her one lit a fire under her ass.

Realistically, we're probably only covering about a mile an hour in this snow. I think we've been walking for around fifteen hours, traveling north of the crash site because that's the direction the plane was flying. I hoped we'd eventually reach civilization, but so far, we've seen nothing but snow and trees.

We could stop at the next densely forested area we find, but I don't think we should. With wet feet, we're on borrowed time. I stop my train of thought as soon as it goes there.

In hockey, if you think you could lose, you're far more likely to. You have to go into a game with a laser focus on doing whatever it takes to win. That's how I'm approaching this situation. It's not about the number of miles or the temperature. It's about my personal drive. No quitting.

I didn't tell Trinity I was hoping rescuers could track us through my phone because I didn't want to get her hopes up. I've got a friend who's an FBI agent and I know they can do some sophisticated shit with phones these days.

I turned the phone off to preserve the battery. Maybe that was the wrong move. Maybe it's already dead anyway.

This can't be the way I go out. There are so many things I never got to do. The pro hockey record that seemed so important a couple of days ago feels completely meaningless now.

Living. That's what matters. Making it through this without either of us losing body parts to frostbite.

I'm worried about Trinity. Pain and exhaustion are taking a toll on her. And while I'll carry her until my legs won't walk another step if I have to, I can't walk a hundred-plus miles in these conditions.

Part of me wants to get out my phone and record a message for my dad if my phone has any life left. There's a chance rescuers will find it and share it with him. But Trinity will know how dire I think things are if I do, and I don't want that.

"Lincoln." Trinity's voice is hoarse, barely audible over the wind. I turn and see her pointing. "Light."

I squint at the faint glow in the distance. How could there be a light out here? Blinking, I try to get a better look at it, but there's snow blowing everywhere.

"I don't know," I say. "You think so?"

"It's a light." Her voice is stronger now. "We have to walk that way."

I guess if there's even a chance, we should do it.

I turn to the right, leading her in the direction she was pointing.

This place is darker and quieter than anywhere I've ever been. There are no city lights. Just the stars. Our heavy breaths are the only sounds until the howl of a distant wolf breaks the near silence.

As we draw closer, my pulse kicks up as I realize Trinity is right. We're walking toward a light. I break into a run, which is really just a faster walk in all the snow. After another quarter of a mile or so, I see that the bright outdoor light is mounted on a pole that's around twenty feet tall. In its glow, I make out the shape of a roofline.

"A building!" I call over my shoulder to Trinity. "There's a building!"

She cries out and starts to hobble-run. Tears burn my eyes as I race the rest of the way to what turns out to be a small cabin. I'm breathless by the time I step onto the front porch, which spans the entire length of the front of the cabin.

I take a few seconds to catch my breath as Trinity makes it to the porch.

"Thank you, thank you, thank you," she says through tears. "Should we knock?"

"Yeah. I didn't see any vehicles, but there might be someone in there."

I approach the front door, lowering my brows when I see that it's locked from the outside by a bar of metal. It looks like if I just lift the bar, I'll be able to open the door.

I pound on the door for a full fifteen seconds, then wait. Nothing. I pound again, this time yelling.

"Hello? Hey, we need some help! Anyone in there?"

When we don't hear a sound in response, Trinity and I exchange a quick glance. I raise the black metal bar and turn the doorknob to open the door.

The sweet scent of cedar greets me as I step inside, a wood floorboard creaking beneath my foot.

"Hello?" I call out. "I'm not an intruder; I just need some help."

The outside light isn't helping in here. I get my phone from my pocket, my hands too cold to push the buttons I need at first.

When I finally get it powered up and turn on the flashlight, I shine it around the room. The cabin is all open, with a bed against one wall, a fireplace, a kitchen area and a bathtub.

There's also a neat little wood rolltop desk with a lamp on top. I walk over and use my phone flashlight to find the little knob on the lamp, turning it.

We're alone here.

The cabin is flooded with dim light and Trinity gasps. A bed and fireplace are more than either of us were even hoping for. She pushes the door closed and drops to her knees, crying.

I'm on the verge of tears myself. Finding this cabin feels like a miracle. It doesn't seem to be heated, but just getting out of the wind is huge.

"Maybe there's a phone." She gets up and limps toward the desk.

"I'll look. You need to lie down."

She looks at the bed and then back at me. I glance at the small love seat in front of the fireplace, which has a folded quilt draped over one arm.

"I'll sleep on the love seat; you take the bed."

"No, we'll share the bed. Both of us need to get out of our wet clothes and get warm. Let's add that quilt to the bed."

I nod, glad she's being practical. As she sits on the edge of the full-size bed and pulls off her wet boots and socks, I look around for a phone but don't find one. I go through all the kitchen drawers and the small chest of drawers standing near the front door.

"Holy shit." There are clothes inside.

I pull out two sets of one-piece thermal underwear and two pairs of socks. When I turn to show Trinity, she's got her left foot up on the bed and I get my first good look at it.

I didn't know it was this bad. Her ankle is swollen to twice its usual size and it's marked with purple bruises. Guilt stabs me in the chest. I pushed her to walk all those miles in this condition. She's right—I am an asshole.

I consolidated most of the contents of the first aid kit into the survival kit, so I'd only have one thing to carry. I open it and take out the nylon wrap.

"You want me to wrap it?"

She shakes her head. "Maybe tomorrow. Did you find dry clothes?"

"Yeah." I walk over to her. "You need some help changing?"

Her cheeks turn pink as she looks up at me. "I can do it. Can you not look, though?"

"Of course I won't look."

I walk over to the wall next to the front door, which has multiple gun racks loaded with different-sized guns, a few hunting knives and even a bow and arrow. Whoever owns this place seems to be a big hunter.

"Ah..." Trinity hisses through her teeth. "God, that hurts."

I keep my back to her as she changes, which sounds like a painful process.

"Okay, I'm decent again," she finally says.

She's wearing white long underwear which is about two sizes too big, the color dull from lots of washings. Even with her blond hair a mess and her face red from the cold, she looks cute.

"Here." I walk over and put an arm around her, supporting her while she stands on her good foot.

I pull down the blankets in the bed and then help her sit down on it. Tears shine in her eyes as she looks up at me.

"Can you believe this?" She smiles.

"You were right about finding shelter." I grab a pair of socks and bend down, helping her get her good foot into one.

"You might've been right, too. Maybe there's a rescue team at the plane right now looking for us."

Her eyelids are drifting closed.

"You want to try a sock on that other foot?"

She shakes her head. "No. I just want to sleep."

I help her tuck her feet beneath the covers and

then cover her up. The bed has sheets and two blankets on it, one of them made of thick wool and the other another worn quilt.

I spread the other quilt out over the bed, suddenly very aware of my wet, freezing feet. I walk around to the other side of the bed and slide off my wet clothes, groaning with happiness as I slide on the dry socks. I step into the long underwear after that and button it up.

There's a pack of matches on the fireplace's rustic wood mantel and a lot of firewood in a small back room of the cabin. I get a fire going and hang up all of our wet clothes, switch off the lamp and climb into bed beside Trinity.

She's already snoring lightly. I close my eyes and exhale fully for what feels like the first time since we set out from the crash site.

I don't know where we are or exactly what will come next, but the worst of the danger is past.

We're going to live.

seven

TRINITY

My mouth feels like someone stuffed it full of cotton. I sit up, my arms aching with the effort of supporting my weight.

"Hey," a deep male voice says from nearby.

Lincoln. I'm so groggy it took me a second to register where we are and how we got here.

Plane crash. Chris. Long, freezing walk. Cabin.

"How long was I asleep?" My voice cracks, my throat so dry it hurts.

"Twelve hours. I was out for about ten." He brings me a clear plastic cup full of water and I take it, drinking the entire thing. "You want more?"

I nod, passing him the cup. "Thanks."

There's light coming in through two small windows, one near the front door and one on the back wall of the cabin. Both windows have heavy wood shutters that bolt closed from the inside, and it looks like Lincoln opened them.

It's a cozy little cabin, other than the wall of weaponry. A fire crackles in the fireplace and several throw rugs cover the rustic wood floor. There's a tiny wood table with a chair on either side of it next to the kitchen area. A beautiful white claw-foot bathtub sits alone in one corner, a little shelf on the wall holding some bubble bath and a few stacked bars of soap.

"Are you hungry?" Lincoln asks as he walks back over to the bed.

I cringe as I swing my legs over the edge of the bed, my ankle throbbing with pain. "How many bars do we have left?"

"You won't believe our luck." He passes me the cup. "The room with the firewood has built-in floor-to-ceiling shelves with canned food and there are two big metal barrels full of rice. And also a bunch of five-gallon containers of water. I think we might have found a prepper's place."

I blink, stunned by the news. "Do you think the owner will mind if we eat some of their food?"

"I'll pay them back several times over for whatever we use."

My body relaxes as I realize for the first time since the crash that we aren't going to die out here.

Lincoln continues. "I took a quick look outside after I woke up earlier and I didn't see any other signs of life. We need to stay here for now so you can rest your ankle."

I slide onto my feet, whimpering as a bolt of pain shoots through my foot and leg. Lincoln is beside me in an instant, putting his arm around my waist so I can take the weight off my left foot.

I feel his solid, muscled body through the fabric of the long underwear. He's warm. As he looks down at me, I suddenly feel self-conscious about not buttoning the one-piece garment all the way up. He's probably getting an unsolicited view of my breasts right now.

"You should stay in bed," he says.

"I have to pee."

He furrows his brow as he realizes he can't argue with me about that. "There's an outhouse around back. I'll help you get out there."

When I cringe, he arches his brows in a look of annoyance. "Would you rather squat in the snow?"

He's such a man. I glare at him. "I can't just whip it out and pee wherever. Is there a seat in the...outhouse?"

Even the word is gross. Might as well just call it a shitter.

"I don't remember. Want to just piss your pants just in case there's no seat?"

"I'd bet my Savings account that you're single," I say lightly as he helps me get into a standing position. "Your looks are canceled out by your personality."

"So you think I'm good-looking?" His voice is loaded with arrogant satisfaction.

"That's what you got out of that?"

"You have been giving me some thirsty looks. Bet you were secretly thrilled to see there's just one bed in here."

I roll my eyes. "This conversation is over."

The cabin has a back door that opens to a wide, mostly enclosed walkway made of concrete blocks. About a foot of it is open at the top of the walls, snowflakes floating in on one side.

This cabin can't be the only one.

"Do you think we're on the edge of a town?" I ask hopefully.

"Hope so."

Walking proves too painful, so I switch to hopping on my good foot. After a single hop, Lincoln sweeps me into his arms, making me gasp with surprise. I open my mouth to protest, but he cuts me off with a grin.

"I know. You're incredibly turned on right now."

"Fuck you. Put me down."

His expression turns serious. "You should be resting your ankle, not walking on it. It's easier this way."

My ankle is in a lot of pain and I have to pee so badly that I don't argue with him.

I'm forced to put my arm around his neck, my heart racing at the intimacy of being carried by him. I have a closeup view of the dark scruff on his face and one of my breasts rests against his chest.

When he opens the door to the outhouse, the butterflies in my stomach come to an immediate halt. The smell in here isn't strong, but there is a stale, unmistakable outhouse odor. He sets me down.

"I'll wait outside the door."

I nod, silently cursing myself for jumping out of that plane. This is a vulnerable position I'm in, needing his help. If not for my injury, we could rest up and push on in search of another cabin, maybe one with other people in it who could call for help.

The deep hole in the ground with a plastic toilet seat on top is better than peeing outside. It even has toilet paper, which is thin, scratchy and, according to the unopened packages stacked by the door, biodegradable.

Lincoln picks me up again, carries me back into the cabin and sets me on the bed.

"Maybe if I take some Tylenol from the first aid kit, my ankle will be good enough to keep walking until we find another cabin."

He scoffs and shakes his head. "Absolutely not. You're staying right here. We were damn lucky to find this place."

I don't like the way he always assumes he's in charge. I started my idea with "maybe if" and, not surprisingly, got shut down with "absolutely not." I take a firmer approach.

"We can't just stay here forever, Lincoln."

His eyes widen with disbelief. "I'm not saying that, but we'd be fools to assume there's a cabin like this just waiting for us every five miles we walk. I don't even know how you made it here on that ankle."

"I had no choice." I glare at him. "And if we want to get home, I still don't."

"Bullshit. We're going to stay here where we're out of the cold. It's fucking January in Alaska."

"I know, but--"

He puts up a hand to stop me. "Look, I'm planning to go out and see if I can find help. I can walk a lot faster by myself. You're staying here."

My pulse pounds with worry. "You're leaving me here alone?"

"How else can I go get help? It's not like I'm not coming back."

I fight back tears, hating the way I cry so easily. "I think we should stay together."

I sound so helpless. But then again, I kind of am the definition of helpless right now.

"We *are* staying together." He gives me the annoyed look an adult would give a misbehaving toddler. "But I'm the better choice to go for help."

I look at the quilt on the bed, forcing myself to stay silent. Though I'd like to tell him to leave right this second, the truth is that I'm scared to be left here alone. He could die out there by himself, and then what?

"You know I'm right," he says.

"I know you want to be the big hero who ventured out in the cold to save our lives. But whatever, it's not like I'm in any position to make you stay. We can go our separate ways."

I move back onto the bed and gingerly lift my foot onto the mattress.

"For fuck's sake, Trinity. It would be a dumbass move for us to both go off walking in different directions."

Even after sleeping for twelve hours, my eyelids still feel heavy. "Look, I'm not in the mood to argue with you. If you're still here when I wake up, I'll talk to you then."

"You need to eat something."

"And you need to stop being such a dick."

I pull the covers up over myself, pain radiating from my ankle. It's hard to keep track of days here with how dark it is most of the time, but I know whatever day it is, everyone is considering the possibility that we're dead.

My mom and Dalton have to be frantic. Someone new will be tasked with leading the Allura launch at work. I know I should be grateful to be alive, and I am, but that launch meant so much to me.

How long will they search for us? When will they give up and hold funerals? The thought of my mom and Dalton at my funeral when I'm not even dead makes me want to laugh and cry at the same time.

And I have no one to voice these worries to. My anxiety means I have a constant running dialogue of worst-case scenarios, and now I don't have my daily medication or my supplemental one for when I'm having an anxiety spike.

It's such irony not having my medications when I've never needed them more.

Is someone feeding my cat Karma? Will the new Allura team leader figure out my system for organizing the materials for each individual product? Will anyone at work even be able to log onto my computer since no one but me knows my password? Is Dalton racked with guilt over putting us on that plane? Does my mom know how sorry I am that I worked instead of coming to see her for her last birthday?

I squeeze my eyes shut as questions fly through my mind at a rapid-fire pace. The only upside to the near-death exhaustion I felt when we got here was that it silenced my nonurgent worries. Now my anxiety has all the energy it needs to run at full capacity.

And I have to hide it from Lincoln. There's no way he'll understand how different my mind is from his. If he knew I was worried about my work computer password, I'm sure I'd get a scowl and a question like, "Are you fucking serious?"

Dealing with my anxiety is hard enough. I don't need his caveman bullshit about it.

eight

LINCOLN

Trinity's been curled up on the bed since I last helped her to the outhouse an hour ago. She hasn't said a word, and I can't get her to tell me what's up.

"I might be gone for twenty-four hours or more," I tell her for the third time as I slide on one of my boots while sitting at the kitchen table. "If you're sick, you need to let me know and I'll wait until tomorrow."

"I'll be fine," she says flatly.

Her usual fire is nowhere to be found and that concerns me. Both of us have slept a lot in the last couple of days. Even though there's plenty of water in the storage room, I figured we should save it, so I've been filling cups, cooking pots and bowls from the kitchen cabinets with snow that we drink when it melts, and we're finally rehydrated.

This trip is going to be a lot smoother than the trip here. I won't have to worry about Trinity, I can wear my coat and I'm layering on extra gear I found in the storage room. The ski mask, heavy gloves and scarf will keep me a lot warmer than the moving pad and emergency blanket did.

My cell phone is dead, but I have a flashlight I found in a kitchen cabinet. I'm also bringing a leather-sheathed hunting knife in case I run into trouble.

"You've got plenty of firewood and water. Is there anything else you need before I go?"

"No, I'm good."

A flare of aggravation makes me exhale heavily. I'm trying to get us rescued, and she's pulling the old *I'm fine* bullshit. All I can do is try. I'm not going to beg her to talk to me.

"I'm heading west. Do not leave this cabin for any reason. I'll be back, so don't come looking for me." When she doesn't respond, I add, "Okay?"

"Stop treating me like a child," she snaps.

"Stop acting like one, then."

She doesn't fire back, which bothers me more than anything. The shell of a person curled up on the bed is not the Trinity I've spent the past few days with. Has she given up?

"We might be out of here by this time tomorrow," I say as I tuck my pant legs into my boots. "We could be a couple miles away from help."

"I hope so."

I put my hand on the doorknob, looking over my shoulder at her. "I'll see you before long. Don't forget to drink lots of water."

"I will. Be careful. Don't run away from bears."

Her random advice makes me lower my brows. "What should I do? Play dead?"

"No. Reason three hundred and twelve this is a bad idea. You have no idea what you're doing. Stand your ground and move away slowly if it's safe. If the bear is acting aggressively toward you, start yelling and try to make yourself look big. That comes pretty naturally to you."

There she is. A smile plays on my lips. "Got it. Hopefully I'll be back soon with help."

No response this time.

I open the door and walk out, making sure it's

closed behind me before I lower the bolt to secure it.

Trinity can be so fucking aggravating. You'd think in this situation we could both let go of any pettiness and focus on surviving, but she's still a woman. Emotional. Maddening.

My last girlfriend and I were together for five months and we argued less than Trinity and I have in a matter of days. We're in stressful circumstances, though. And Sarah agreed with me on pretty much everything. She didn't have any ideas or opinions of her own, and ultimately my boredom with her was the reason we broke up.

Trinity would argue with me about twenty of twenty things I said if she didn't agree with me. She won't think this trip out was a bad idea anymore when I come back with help. Hell, she'll probably say it was *her* idea if it works out.

It's still cold as fuck, and the dark doesn't help. The wind is only hitting my eyes and lips, thanks to the ski mask, though.

Snow crunches under my boots as I walk. I wonder if searchers have found the plane and Chris's remains yet. Maybe they're tracking us to the cabin right now. My team can't take a break from the schedule for any reason, even a missing team member. I wish I knew what adjustments Coach made to the roster to compensate for my absence.

This is horrible timing. We're in playoff contention and I was closing in on a team record. I never realized how much noise there was in my life until I ended up in this eerily silent place. I'm used to screaming crowds, locker room conversation, the buzz of crowded bars and restaurants. The only silence in my life is usually when I'm sleeping.

My plan is to walk as far as I can unless the wind picks up and the snow starts drifting. I have to be able to follow my footprints to get back. I already know there's nothing in the direction we came from, so hopefully this one will lead me to someone. Anyone with a phone will do.

Since my mom passed away, I don't have family who are worried about me. Maybe my dad, if he sees a story on the news about the plane crash. It's been more than twenty years since he saw me, though. My teammates are my family now, and I imagine not knowing if your team captain survived a plane crash puts a dark cloud over the locker room. Hopefully they can push through and still win.

I smile beneath my ski mask at the expanse of

sparkling, untouched snow ahead. It kind of looks like a fresh ice rink. Full of possibility.

How long do people have to be missing before they're declared dead? I don't think we're anywhere close to that. It has to be at least a few months, I'm sure.

I plan to be back home in time to help my team clinch that playoff spot. That record's still going to be mine, and it'll be even more special after this unplanned detour.

We're still in the United States, for fuck's sake. It's not like we crashed in some remote jungle. Either help will arrive, or I'll find it.

If there's one thing everyone who knows me would say about Lincoln Rowe, it's that when I put my mind to something, I'm hard as fuck to stop.

I'm getting back to my team. And saving Trinity's stubborn, moody ass.

nine

TRINITY

I CLOSE MY EYES, FIGHTING TO KEEP DOWN THE water I just drank. Between nausea and my pounding headache, I'm miserable. I've slept as much as I can, so now I'm forced to just lie here, worries swirling through my mind.

I knew serotonin withdrawal could be physically rough, but I didn't know it would also make me so emotional. My doctor has told me about the importance of slowly tapering off my medication if I ever decide to go off of it, and I always laugh and tell her there's no way I'll ever go off of it. It changed my life for the better.

And then my plane crashed, so here I am, in withdrawal from the medication that helps lessen my anxiety symptoms. Just crying and wishing I had someone to rage at.

I'm too embarrassed to tell Lincoln what's wrong with me. I'm hoping my symptoms will pass soon. In the meantime, I'd do anything for a distraction.

This cabin is such a mystery to me. Lincoln said there are solar panels on the roof, which explains the electricity that powers the outdoor light, the lamp, an outlet in the kitchen, and the vintage-looking record player that sits atop a wood cabinet with an open shelf that holds vinyl records.

Someone went to a lot of trouble to build this place. How did they get all those concrete blocks here for the long walkway to the outhouse? Who is all the food for?

This place has primitive-looking wood floors, but I'm almost positive the large rug beneath the bed with a large butterfly on it is an Alexander McQueen. Those rugs have five and six-figure price tags, which I only know because my boss whispered it to me when we saw one in the Kiss My Sass CEO's office.

And then there's the bathtub with no plumbing.

Not that plumbing is possible in a place that gets this cold. I'd love to take a bath, but the only way I can see to use the tub is to melt or thaw snow and fill it one bowl or bucket at a time.

Right now, between my ankle and the serotonin withdrawal, I could manage to put maybe half an inch of cold water in it.

Being rescued seems like too much to hope for, but I daydream about it constantly. The thought of a helicopter landing in front of the cabin and whisking us the hell out of here would feel like winning the lottery would have felt pre–plane crash.

My standards have already shifted so much. I cringe to think of all the times I lamented returning to work on Monday morning after a great weekend. Poor Trin, drinking a hot Starbucks in a nice warm office, freshly showered and able to call anyone at any time. A hot ham and cheese from the deli near my office would change my life right now. How many of those sandwiches did I mindlessly scarf?

Lincoln has been keeping a fire going night and day, getting up every couple of hours even when he's sleeping. It's still cold in the cabin, but I stay bundled up or under the covers. He makes sure I have plenty of water and never complains about carrying me to the bathroom.

Like the cabin, he's a mystery. He goes out of his way to take care of me and I know he's a nice guy, but he's also easily irritated. Every time he gets in on the other side of the bed to sleep, he stays on his side and keeps his back to me.

Sometimes I wish he'd turn over and face me. Pull me into his arms. I don't know if it's my anxiety seeking comfort or if it's a genuine attraction I'm feeling for him. Either way, his hard chest and strong arms tempt me day and night.

I limp over to the record player and pull out a record. It's a Frank Sinatra, which makes me smile. My grandpa loved him. We used to dance to Sinatra music in his kitchen when Dalton and I spent time at our grandparents' house during the summer.

It doesn't take long for me to figure out the record player and drop the needle onto the record. When I hear the first notes of "Blue Skies," tears fill my eyes. I can practically hear my grandpa's laugh and smell the breakfast pancakes cooking.

Suddenly I don't feel so alone. The headache and nausea are still there, but now they aren't the only thing I have to focus on. I slowly make my way back to the bed, force down another sip of water, and lie down on my back, hoping the soothing sound of Frank Sinatra's voice might ease my headache.

I WAKE UP WITH A GASP, MY HEART POUNDING IN response to my recurring dream I'm drowning. I'm in the cabin and it's completely dark.

"Lincoln?" I croak, my throat dry.

When he doesn't respond, I get out of bed and limp over to the lamp, fumbling for the switch. Dim light fills the room and my gaze goes to the fireplace. The fire is completely out.

Lincoln hasn't returned. Anxious dread freezes me in place for a few seconds. I still haven't shaken the effects of the dream and it's ice cold inside the cabin, wind whipping against the outside walls and windows.

I walk over to the fireplace and get the fire going again, then close and latch the wood shutters for both windows.

Why didn't I push harder for him to stay here or to go with him? He might be freezing to death in the snow right now, lost.

Before he left, he told me to drink plenty of water. I told him yelling and acting big come naturally to him. I cringe as I realize how ungrateful I must seem to him when the truth is I wouldn't be alive without him.

Sarcasm is a defense mechanism for me, but he doesn't know that. He probably thinks I'm just a cranky bitch.

That makes me laugh for some reason. My coworker and best friend, Genevieve, always says we're cranky bitches. She'd say I'm entitled to be cranky right now, but Lincoln is staying mentally tough and I wish I could do the same. I want to be an asset to him, not a liability.

I wipe a tear from my cheek and go over to the record player, where I switch out the record for an Ella Fitzgerald. Her strong, smooth voice immediately comforts me and makes me feel less alone.

My headache and nausea are ever present, but I make myself stay upright instead of crawling back into bed. I drink a couple cups of water and go to the outhouse to pee, then settle onto the love seat with one of the paperbacks from a single shelf on the wall.

My gaze keeps wandering from the words on the pages to the cabin door. All I want is for Lincoln to walk through that doorway, his massive frame filling it before he scowls at me about something.

I can get through withdrawal from my medication. I'll find a way to cope with my situation without it, somehow.

But I'd much rather do it with Lincoln than alone.

ten

LINCOLN

I HUFF OUT AN AGGRAVATED SIGH WHEN I SEE THE snowdrift blocking the cabin door.

Awesome. I'm freezing and exhausted from walking for what felt like at least twelve hours. Not to mention cranky as shit from not finding a damn thing other than more snow and trees. And now I have to dig my way inside.

There's a snow shovel leaning against the cabin near the front door, which helps. I scoop and throw enough snow to get the door open, breathing hard when I put the shovel back.

It's different exercise than I'm used to, but at

least I'm staying active. That'll help me get right back on the ice when I get home.

When I open the door, Trinity turns and looks at me from in front of the fireplace, where she's using the metal poker to move wood around and stoke the fire.

"Hey." She smiles. "I was hoping that was you out front and not a bear."

She's changed out of the long underwear and is now wearing black leggings and a men's flannel that's oversized on her. For a second, I imagine we're at a five-star lodge for a long weekend of skiing, about to settle onto the love seat with some wine. I'd offer her a foot rub and my hands would roam up her calves, to her thighs and then...

"Did you find anything?" she asks, standing.

"No." I drop my gloves, hat and scarf, then take off my coat and add it to the pile. "Thanks for keeping the fire going."

I go over to the fireplace and crouch down, holding my hands out to warm them up. The warmth makes me want to groan with satisfaction. I started fantasizing about this around hour four of walking.

Trinity sits down on the end of the bed. "Sorry

about my mood earlier. I have a headache, but I shouldn't have taken it out on you."

"It's okay." I glance at the kitchen area. "Have you eaten anything?"

"I had some peanut butter."

My stomach growls just from the sound of it. "Hell yes. I could eat an entire jar. I'm dying for some protein."

"There's beef jerky in the storage room. Do you want me to get you some?"

I stand. "No, you should rest that ankle. I'll get it."

When I reach the storage room, I scan the well-organized shelves. Most of the items have labels. Rice. Oatmeal. Beans. As soon as my eyes land on the plastic containers of beef jerky, I grab one and tear it open, taking some out and biting into it.

This time, I do groan with satisfaction. The savory flavor of the meat is intensified by my hunger. I'm beat; I need food, water and sleep before I can think about our next step.

"Was it pretty rough out there?" Trinity asks.

This cabin is so small that she's not very far away even though we're in different rooms. I step back and look through the doorway so she's in my line of sight.

"Yeah. I didn't see a damn thing."

She gets up and limps over to the record player. "Want me to put on some music?"

"Sure."

I'm so tired I could sleep through a live Metallica concert, so I don't care what she picks. Still, I find myself surprised when she chooses Nat King Cole.

"What I wouldn't give for a working faucet on that bathtub," she cracks.

Her blond hair is loose around her shoulders. The feeling that we could easily be here on a date returns. When Trinity's smiling at me instead of snarling, she's actually beautiful. I was deliberately avoiding thinking about it before, because she's Dalton's little sister.

Now that we're alone here, though, I find myself intrigued by what she's like beneath her sometimes prickly shield.

I bury the thought because I can't go there. No matter our circumstances, she's still my teammate's sister. I'll protect her and take care of her, but that's it.

"It looks like there's a heating element in there," I say, pouring myself a glass of water. "That has to be what the switch is for. After I get some sleep, I'll fill it with water, and we'll see if we can figure out how to heat it up."

She gapes at me. "Really? A hot bath would be heavenly. Even a lukewarm one. Anything, really, just to get clean."

I imagine her undoing the flannel buttons one at a time, her eyes locked on mine as I watch her.

Fuck me. I just shut that line of thought down thirty seconds ago and it's creeping back in. I force myself to look away from her and drink my water. When I finish and glance at her, she's rubbing her temple, her expression one I know all too well.

I've seen teammates try to mask their pain to stay in games. Hell, I've done it myself. And that headache Trinity mentioned has to be a doozy from the look on her face.

"Hey, can I give you a little hockey player advice?" I say as I walk over to her.

Looking puzzled, she says, "Sure."

"Dehydration is a major cause of headaches. Even if you think you've been drinking a lot of water, with all the walking we did, it might not be enough. Take some Tylenol and drink enough water that you have to pee every hour. It'll help."

She nods. "I will. And I'll keep the fire going while you sleep. You haven't gotten more than a couple of hours in a row since we got here because of the fire."

"Thanks."

I can't manage more than that word because I'm so exhausted. My T-shirt is sweaty in places from my walk and I don't have the energy to change from my jeans into the long underwear. Instead, I just pull my T-shirt off, drop it to the floor beside the bed and climb in, jeans and all.

I feel myself falling asleep within a minute.

WHEN I WAKE UP, MY NOSE IS COLD BUT I'M WARM from the neck down, buried in covers. I raise my head from the pillow a few inches and see Trinity curled up on the love seat, engrossed in a book. The fire is going strong and music is playing at a low volume.

It's dark outside, but that doesn't tell me much about the time here since it's dark so much of the time.

When I sit up, Trinity looks over at me. "Hey. Feel better?"

I scrub a hand down my face, still groggy. "Yeah. How long did I sleep?"

She looks at the small clock on the fireplace mantel. "Ten hours."

"Damn." I get out of bed and grab my shirt from the floor. "How's your headache?"

There's a quick pause before she says, "It's better."

I can tell she's bluffing, but there's a glass of water on the little table beside the love seat, so at least she's drinking water.

After I hit the outhouse, I drink some water myself. Our snow-supplied water is getting low. Probably time to get out one of the five-gallon jugs. I realized while I was walking that the smartest thing is to drink water from one of them and then refill it with melted snow. Then I won't have to fill every pot, bowl and cup in the cabin.

My stomach growls and Trinity laughs lightly.

"I heard that all the way over here. Why don't I make us some rice and we can eat an actual meal?"

"Yeah, I'm down for that. I'll start filling the tub while you do that."

Her smile lights up her entire face, making me feel like I just won a prize. I don't know why I'm finding it so damn hard to turn off my attraction for her. Denying it may be impossible, but I won't act on it.

"Thank you." She gets up from the couch and limps to the storage room.

Even with the biggest pot the cabin's kitchen has, it's going to take me a long fucking time to fill up the tub. And then the snow has to melt, which will move faster if the heating element works.

Is this what the cabin's owner does? I'm starting to think this cabin has never gotten much use. Maybe someone built it as an escape if the world goes to shit, and they've never actually had to fill this tub.

Trinity's busy at the kitchen stove, my gaze wandering to her every time I bring in a pot of snow to dump in the tub. I catch a glimpse of her expression and sense again that something's wrong.

She's in more pain than she's letting on, but I don't know if it's from her ankle or her headache.

"Hey, why don't you sit back down and I'll finish that?" I say.

She turns to look at me. "No, I'm okay."

I should accept her answer and return to filling the tub, but I hate the thought of her hurting.

"It doesn't bother me at all, you know. If I'm doing more than you are. You've got a jacked ankle and a headache."

"I'm fine. Keeping busy helps me push past it. Just lying in bed all the time isn't good for me."

I set down the pot and walk over to her. "Helps you push past what? Is it the ankle or the headache?"

A flicker of annoyance passes over her expression. "I said I'm fine."

What's with her? Why won't she just tell me what's bothering her?

"If there's something going on with you, I need to know about it."

She scoffs. "Why?"

"Because...we're in this together."

She takes a deep breath, pinching her brows together. "I'm trying to be in a better mood, okay? And while I've felt better, we were in a plane crash almost a week ago. I think eating might help, so I'm going to finish making our food."

I nod, not liking it but trying to give her space. The lack of food has taken a toll on me, so maybe that's what's going on with her, too. I don't think so, though. It's all I can do not to tell her to strip down so I can inspect every inch of her and make sure she doesn't have an infected cut somewhere or something.

Nothing is as simple here as it would be at

home. I can't take her to a hospital for antibiotics. But I can't force her to tell me what's going on, either. All I can do is wait, which isn't easy for me. I solve problems and never avoid dealing with things head-on.

Fighting won't help anything, though, so I return to filling the tub. About half an hour later, Trinity announces that it's time to eat.

I sit at the kitchen table, my mouth watering when she sets down a plate of hot white rice covered with chili. Her plate only has about a cup of rice and a cup of dried bananas.

"You need protein," I tell her.

She shakes her head. "This is what I'm eating. I don't think the chili would agree with my stomach."

"But--"

She cuts me off. "Let's just eat, Lincoln."

I hold her gaze for a few seconds, something I see in her eyes making me back down. "Call me Linc. All my friends do."

She sits down. "Am I your friend?"

I grin at her. "With this meal, you just became my best friend. How'd you do this?"

"With the hot plate I found in one of the kitchen cabinets. It took forever to boil the water and cook the rice, and it's just canned chili, but it's better than beef jerky and protein bars."

"Much better. Thanks for making it."

"Thanks for the bathwater."

"It's heating up right now."

She smiles. "I can't wait."

The first bite of my first hot meal in nearly a week doesn't disappoint. I nod with approval and we both eat in silence for a minute. Trinity made me an enormous plate and I plan to eat every last morsel.

"I'll go out again tomorrow," I say. "I figure I'll try a different direction."

She nods, her expression telling me she's not a big fan of the idea.

"I saw a plane overhead when I was out. It was too far up for anyone to see me."

"Do you think it was the search party?"

I shrug. "It could have been a commercial plane, I don't know."

"At least we have a safe place to wait it out," she murmurs. "And plenty of food."

She nibbles at the food, only half of it gone by the time I'm finished with my entire plate. My concern for her is at the front of my mind. Something's not right.

My only chance to look her over for injuries might be when she's taking a bath. I don't want to look like a perv, but I have to know if she's hurt. An infection while stuck here would be serious. I'm not sure what I'll do if I find out she's got something going on that needs quick treatment, but it's not knowing that's making me crazy right now.

"You should eat the rest of that," I tell her, nodding toward her half-empty plate.

"I can't."

"Why not? We're literally starving here."

"I'm just not hungry for more." She picks up both of our plates and takes them over to the counter. "I'm going to wash these and then take a bath."

I press my lips together, willing myself not to argue with her. We've got to get along, or we'll both be miserable.

Whatever's going on with her, I'm going to have to figure it out on my own.

eleven

TRINITY

"COULD YOU MAYBE…WAIT IN THE OUTHOUSE?"

Lincoln gapes at me, clearly not on board with the idea. "The outhouse? It's cold as shit out there."

"I can make it fast. Ten minutes?"

He lowers his brows, consternation written all over his face. "It took me an hour to fill that tub, and you want to take a ten-minute bath?"

I'm in no mood to bicker with him. My headache hasn't budged an inch and the fatigue and nausea have gotten even worse.

"No, I'd love to sit in there for an hour, but not with you watching me."

"Who said I'm going to watch you?" he snaps. "I can keep my eyes to myself."

I sigh heavily. "I know you wouldn't gawk or anything, but you could accidentally glance over."

"I won't."

My hot bubble bath is standing by and it's been so long since I bathed that I can smell myself, making his stubbornness an even sharper thorn in my side. "Would you want to get naked in front of someone you just met a week ago?"

He shrugs. "I'll take my clothes off right now if it'll make you feel better."

"It wouldn't." Why is he so exasperating? "You've gotten naked in front of hundreds of people. Or maybe thousands? But I'm modest and I've only been naked in front of like...two people. Can you understand that?"

A grin tugs at his lips. "Thousands?"

"Come on, you know I'm not far off."

"I mean, if you're counting all the guys who have seen me naked in the locker room...it's still not in the thousands. I'm not the manwhore you seem to think I am."

"I just want to take a bath." There's a pleading note in my tone.

His expression turns serious. "I'll sit on the bed with my back to you the entire time."

I feel so awful and the bath looks so inviting that I give up. "Fine. But if I catch you looking at me, you're sleeping in the outhouse tonight."

He puts his palms up. "I'm not going to look, Trin."

There's something intimate about the way he shortens my name. We've gotten to know each other well in a short amount of time. Facing death with someone quickly shows you who they really are, and I've never had that experience with anyone else.

I'd never admit it out loud, but it would secretly thrill me to know Lincoln even considered checking me out while I was undressing. I guess being stranded in a cabin with a caveman has shown me that cavemen aren't without their good points.

Like muscles. And tenacity. Lincoln is undeniably physically attractive, but his concern for me is also very appealing. I have no doubt that if I felt like staying in bed all the time, he'd bring me food, help me to the outhouse, keep the fire going and look for help with no complaints.

He's a real man, and he's kept his word on everything else, so I trust that he won't peek at me while I'm undressing, either.

My gaze stays fixed on his broad back as I quickly slide out of my leggings and underwear. I unbutton the flannel, hesitating for a second before taking it off and then unfastening my bra and dropping it to the floor, too.

When I step into the water, my happy sigh has a twinge of a moan in it. Sitting down hurts my aching body, but once I'm settled in, it feels divine. The tub is deep and perfectly shaped, covering me with bubbles and hot water to my neck once I sink down and lay my head on the edge.

"I could live here," I say, closing my eyes. "Thank you for this, Linc."

"I'm glad you like it. Don't drain it when you're done; I'm going to get in there."

Oh. My brows shoot up. We're going to share the bath. Well, not exactly *share* it, but he's going to use the same water. It's a practical choice, but it feels...close, like something a couple would do.

"Will it stay hot?" I ask him.

"Wh—uh, what?"

"The water? Will it stay hot for you?"

"Oh. Don't worry about that. I can heat it up again and all I want to do is wash off."

I perch my feet on the end of the tub, bubbles covering more than half of my exposed skin. "You should really consider sitting in some bubbles for a while. It's so relaxing."

He shakes his head. "I just want to wash up."

I'm a terrible person for teasing him, but I do. There's a note of breathiness in my voice as I say, "It feels so good."

Lincoln's back goes rigid on the bed. He doesn't respond.

The more I look at the lines of his broad shoulders and carved arm muscles, the more I want him to not sleep with his back to me tonight. I'd love to lie in the crook of his arm, feel his warmth and snuggle against him.

I crave the comfort of him. It's lousy feeling so sick, and being in his arms would help. Unless...he's taken.

"Do you have a girlfriend?" I ask him.

"What? Why are you asking me that?"

He's flustered. Mr. I'm In Charge Here is *flustered* by my question. It makes me smile.

"Just making conversation," I say lightly. "What else is there to do around here?"

"No, I don't have a girlfriend."

"When's the last time you did have one?"

He exhales heavily. "I don't know, like a year and a half ago."

"Wow, that's a long time."

"Being on the road doesn't make for good relationships."

"It must be lonely."

"It's too busy to get lonely. I'm surrounded by my team every minute of the day."

I unwrap a bar of soap and put it in the water, then lather it between my hands. "You probably don't snuggle with them, though."

He responds with a single note of laughter. "Nope, no snuggling with the team."

I wash my face first, then sit up, my eyes locked on his back as I rub soapy lather over my neck, chest and breasts.

"What about you? Do you have a boyfriend back home?"

"No. I hadn't even been on a date in more than a year when I went out with Ronan. I regret saying yes to him, obviously."

"How long did you guys date?"

"We went out twice."

"No shit? That's it?"

I continue washing my body, realizing I haven't thought about the Ronan situation at all since the plane crash. "Yeah, that's it."

"How'd you guys meet?"

"In line at a coffee shop."

He grunts in response, and I can't read the meaning of it. I submerge my head in the water to wet it and then grab the shampoo from the shelf next to the tub. When I see the label—Philip B Amber Imperial Shampoo—I blurt out, "Holy shit."

"What?" Lincoln turns his head to the side and I cry out, plunging myself back into the water.

"Don't look! That was just my reaction to this shampoo. It's a crazy expensive brand."

"Oh."

"I feel bad even using this."

"Don't. I'll pay the cabin owner back for everything we use."

I smile as I open the shampoo. Again, he's making me feel like we're an us. I've never truly been part of an us. My first boyfriend, who I met in college, went to a different school than I did, so we didn't spend a lot of time together. My second boyfriend was an attorney who worked crazy hours and we only saw each other once or twice a week.

"Maybe I can write a guest blog for a beauty magazine after this," I say as I lather my hair. "Best beauty products to use when you're stranded in the wilderness."

He hums his amusement. "Probably not many people in that situation."

"True. This shampoo smells like heaven."

I close my eyes, breathing in the warm amber scent mingled with the coconut-scented bubble bath. With the crackle of the blazing fire, this feels like a luxury spa.

At least until I open my eyes again. Lincoln is still sitting with his back to me, looking at nothing but the cabin wall.

"I'm craving a chocolate shake," he says.

"That sounds incredible. With six inches of whipped cream on top."

I wash, rinse and condition my hair, feeling more like myself than I have since the crash. If I was alone in the cabin, I'd sit here for a long time, but I feel bad about Linc staring at the wall.

I've put my hands on the sides of the tub, ready to get out, when I realize I forgot something crucial.

"I don't have a towel."

"I can get you one. Where are they?"

My heart races at the thought of him seeing me naked. How could I forget about a towel?

"I don't know. I haven't seen any."

There's a second of silence before he says, "Want me to look in the storage room?"

"No! Stay where you are. I'll figure it out."

I sit up in the tub, crossing my arms over my chest and looking around. There's nothing within my reach but the little rug next to the tub.

"There are dish towels in the kitchen," Linc offers. "In the drawer by the coffee maker."

I can't walk across the cabin while soaking wet. I'd get the floors wet and have to turn my back to him to get the towels. I briefly consider just living in the bathtub forever.

"Will you blindfold yourself and get me a couple of towels?"

He scoffs, amused. "No. I could trip over something and hurt myself and I'm the only able-bodied person here."

Good point. I sigh softly.

"Hey Trin, are you covered in scales or something?"

I furrow my brow. "No."

"I'm not going to look, and even if I did, you've got a great body."

My lips part and my pulse pounds, my inner feminist wilting at how good his compliment makes me feel.

"It's not about whether you'd like it. I'm a private person."

"Do you want me to get you the towels or not?"

I sink down below the water's surface from the neck down again. "Yes. Throw them over here or something."

He moves from the bed, my gaze tracking him as he walks across the cabin to the kitchen and gets out two towels. Looking down at the ground, he approaches me, my heart hammering like a drum.

Half of me wants him to look and half of me doesn't. He shields his eyes as he drops the two towels onto the rug beside the bathtub.

I quickly get out of the tub as he stands next to the bed, his back to me.

"Hey, I'd never sneak a look at you taking a bath or make a move on you," he says out of nowhere. "I'm not like that."

His words are more disappointing than I would have expected.

"Oh. Are you gay?"

He laughs softly. "No. I'm just not a guy who takes advantage of situations. You're Dalton's sister and he trusts me with you."

I side-eye his back as I finish drying myself and put my clothes back on. I'm not going to argue with him because I'd have no dignity left by the end of that conversation. If he doesn't see me as a grown woman capable of making my own decisions, I'm not going to try to change his mind.

"Bath is all yours," I say, grabbing my book and limping over to the bed to lie down.

It takes every ounce of my self-control not to sneak even one look as he undresses and bathes, but I force myself not to. I want him to think it's because I'm not interested in what he looks like.

Even though it's a complete lie and I'm still daydreaming about lying against his shoulder, his arm wrapped around my back.

twelve

LINCOLN

TRINITY'S LYING ON HER BACK, STARING UP AT THE ceiling. Though she's been putting on a smile more, I catch her looking miserable when she doesn't know I'm looking. Sleep and food don't seem to be helping her much. I've gotten glimpses of the feisty woman I boarded the plane with just over a week ago, but she's not completely herself.

I was planning to go back out looking for help today, but I don't feel right leaving her when she's sick.

"Have you ever been anemic?" I ask her as I sip a cup of coffee from the love seat.

"Anemic? No, why do you ask?"

Should I be honest? I know she won't like it, but I'm frustrated with trying to figure out how bad she's feeling because she won't just tell me.

"Anemia can cause fatigue."

She sighs heavily. "I'm fine. It's not like I can catch up on work emails, dude. I literally have nothing to do."

"You don't want to read anymore?"

"I've already read the books that interest me."

I set my mug on the coffee table and stand up, stretching. "Want to do some bodyweight exercises with me? I can modify everything for your ankle."

"No, thanks."

I run a hand over the short beard I've grown over the past week. "We have to stay mentally and physically strong, Trin."

"Please don't."

"Don't what?" I pinch my brows together in confusion.

"Don't try to be my team captain. I'm not a hockey player you need to motivate to win a game."

I roll my eyes. "I'm not doing that. I'm just concerned about you. The fatigue, the headache, the mood swings--"

"Mood swings?" She sits up and glares at me.

I fight back a smile. "Yeah, like just then, when you went from calm to pissed off in three seconds."

She shakes her head. "That's not a mood swing; it's *you.*"

I ignore her and keep pushing on what's going on with her. "It's not caffeine withdrawal after a week; that would be over by now."

"Will you just drop it?"

"Do I really seem like the type who drops things?"

"Why don't you do your exercises and burn off some energy?"

I pick up my mug and take a sip. "I will, but first, I want to know what all of your symptoms are."

"No thanks, Dr. Dickhead."

She's the definition of headstrong. This time, I'm not giving up, though. If there's something serious going on with her, I need to know what it is.

"You do realize that in the past twenty-four hours, you've cooked me a meal, flirted with me, yelled at me, thanked me and called me a dickhead?"

Her lips part and for a couple of seconds, she seems too shocked to speak. "*Flirted* with you? You arrogant asshole."

"Oh, come on. We both know you were teasing me during your bath last night. Talking about how good it felt in that sexy voice, asking me if I have a girlfriend."

She balks. "That was me being polite. How could you possibly have a girlfriend when you treat women like this?"

I set the mug down again, walking over to the bed. "I'll stop pushing your buttons if you'll just tell me what's wrong with you."

She gets out of bed and stands face to face with me, having to tilt her head back to meet my eyes because of our height difference.

"What's wrong with me is you." Angry tears fill her eyes and I feel a stab of guilt. "You bitch when I'm in a bad mood and accuse me of flirting with you when I'm in a good mood. I can't win."

I try a softer approach. "I see you cringing when you don't know I'm looking. It's making me crazy not knowing what's going on with you. Will you just tell me? I don't care if it's a...I don't know, a menstrual thing or whatever, just tell me."

Her laugh is unamused. "A menstrual thing." She presses against her temple. "Look, I'm sure this will pass soon. And in the meantime, I'm fine."

Exasperated, I finally blow. "Fucking talk to me!

I'm responsible for your safety and I can't help you if--"

"It's serotonin withdrawal, okay? That's why I'm sick. I've been on medication for anxiety for years and it was in my bag when the plane went down. Any other deeply personal things you feel entitled to know about me?"

I close my eyes and drop my chin, feeling like the world's biggest asshole. "Fuck. I'm sorry."

"I've never been so sick," she says, sounding defeated. "It's hard to eat and I feel horrible, plus my anxiety is raging."

I shake my head and meet her gaze. "You don't have to tell me anything more. I was wrong to push you like that."

She shrugs. "You know now, so at least I can stop pretending I'm fine."

I left her to go look for help when she needed me here. She was sick and probably helpless and I just left. That's even worse than the way I pushed her to reveal something personal.

Now that I know what's going on, though, I no longer have a lead ball of dread in my stomach. It's not something life-threatening.

"How can I help?" I ask.

"Stop being such an asshole?" A smile quirks on her lips.

I laugh. "I deserved that."

She takes a deep breath. "There's nothing you can do. I'm hoping the serotonin withdrawal will pass soon, and then I just have to do my best to cope with my anxiety until we get out of here."

We're standing so close I can see all the shades of her eyes—dark green with flecks of amber and brown. Her long hair is loose around her shoulders and I feel an urge to reach out and touch a section of it.

She's Dalton's sister, though. I have to remind myself of that several times in a row as she looks up at me, her vulnerability so sexy it's making me hard. I want to be there for her, but I have to draw the line at things turning physical.

"You can talk to me," I say softly. "About your anxiety. Or whatever. When I got drafted to my first team, one of my teammates had depression and anxiety. I saw what a bitch it can be."

She looks down and then back up. "I didn't want you to know because you're so strong. I already feel so weak from my ankle. I don't contribute much."

My hand itches to reach out and cup her cheek, but I can't. One touch won't be enough.

"You're not weak," I assure her. "We're in this together every step of the way."

Her expression softens. "I'm sorry about the mood swings. And about irrationally denying them."

Damn. She's a dangerous mix of cute and sexy. I want to pick her up and kiss her until she wraps her legs around me. Get in bed with her and use my mouth and hands to make her forget about feeling sick because she's so turned on.

"Anyway." She clears her throat and looks away. "Are you leaving soon to go look for help?"

"Thought maybe I'd wait another day. That okay with you?"

She nods. "Of course. It looks pretty windy out there. I don't want your tracks to get blown over."

"I won't go out when it's windy."

She sits back down on the bed. "It's hard not having anything to do. I'd give anything for a day packed with conference calls and meetings."

"Will you try something with me?"

Her cheeks flush. "I guess that depends on what it is."

I can think of many dirty things I'd love to try

with her, but I can't, so I shove the thoughts away. "I work with a mindset coach and we do mindfulness meditation. You want to try it?"

"Sure, why not?"

"Okay, so we need to sit across from each other. Let's do it on the bed because of your ankle."

We both get comfortable and I take a few seconds to remember how my mindset coach, Jen, starts these sessions. I used to be dismissive of mindset coaching, but then I started to see the improvements it was making in my life, both on and off the ice.

"Clear your mind of distractions and think about somewhere that feels peaceful to you," I say. Picture that place and then we're going to do some breathing where we inhale for three, hold for two, and exhale for four. Breathe deeply. Put a hand right here." I take her palm and place it beneath her breasts, my thumb brushing over the curve of one breast.

Her eyes flare open slightly from my touch, and I start to get hard again. I foresee a lot of jerking off going down in the outhouse while we're stuck here.

"You want to feel your chest moving in and out

as you breathe. Just focus on that and on the counting."

She moistens her lips with the tip of her tongue and I let my mind roam for just a second, imagining myself lunging toward her to kiss her and press her down against the mattress.

She's twenty-six and if only two people have seen her naked, I imagine they were both sexual partners. I already know her well enough to know she's uptight in bed. Fuck, how I'd love to bring her to the brink over and over with edging, making her tell me what she wants in order to finally get it.

"I'm ready, Linc," she says softly.

"Right." I shake myself out of the daydream, hoping she can't see my erection.

At least I've got jeans on instead of the damned long underwear. I sleep with my back to her every night, so I don't have to worry about her waking up and finding my hard dick poking the bedcovers into the air. Or worse, touching her when I'm on my side facing her.

"Okay, we're going to inhale for one...two...three." I keep my hand on hers to make sure her chest is rising and falling. "Hold for one...two. Now a long exhale. One...two...three...four."

She closes her eyes as I count and she breathes. It's a heady sensation, having her trust me with the knowledge she has anxiety and being allowed to help her manage it. When we were thrown together in this situation, she was forced to rely on me, but now she's choosing to.

I'm past the locked gate she puts up to protect herself, and it makes me want to throw my own gate open and let her see me, too.

Dalton's face appears in my mind, and I imagine myself having to tell him the team captain and friend he trusts like a brother fucked his younger sister when she was in a vulnerable place.

Many times. Because it definitely wouldn't just be once.

I can't do it. I mean, I *could*, but I won't. I'm a better man than that.

I'll just have to find a way to resist my primal urges toward Trinity while we're trapped together in a one-room cabin. With one bed. And a bathtub she likes to soak naked in.

Fuck.

thirteen

TRINITY

Linc gives me an approving look as I finish eating the bowl of oatmeal he made me for breakfast.

"Feeling better?" he asks.

"Yes. I felt like I was about thirty percent myself for the past few days, and today, it's more like sixty. My headache is almost gone."

"Good."

"The brown sugar and raisins in that oatmeal were really good."

"The only thing that was missing was some

really good butter. When we make it back home, I'll make you a bowl with butter, too, and you'll see."

I smile, thinking about home and how much I miss it. "Home's two different places for us, though."

He cringes. "You must hate living in Chicago."

"Not at all, I love it there."

"It's a fun city to visit, but it's too much for me. Traffic's crazy."

"Yeah, I have a car but I don't really drive it except for weekends."

He leans back against the kitchen counter, crossing his arms over his chest. I try not to look too thirsty as I check out his arms, the definition of his muscles showing through the gray thermal shirt he's wearing.

"What's your place like?" he asks me.

"My apartment?" I laugh lightly. "It's tiny. I live downtown and apartments are stupid expensive there. It's a one-bedroom and my bed is lofted to make room for my desk beneath it. My living room and kitchen are small and overflowing with plants. Karma has a cat hammock in the living room window where she lies all day and passes judgment on everyone who walks by."

"What color is Karma?"

"She's the most beautiful shade of gray." I walk over to the sink with my breakfast bowl and spoon. "What about you? Do you live in a brothel?"

He grins. "Not even close, smart-ass. I have a house on the outskirts of Minneapolis."

"Is it furnished, or are you one of those bed, big screen and recliner guys?"

"Fully furnished. I've even got two guest rooms."

I arch my brows, impressed. "Look at you, hosting people. Do you leave clean towels stacked on the bed and a chocolate on their pillows?"

"Fuck no. My housekeeper makes the beds and all that."

I use snow water to rinse my dishes in the sink. "Dalton refuses to stay the night with me when he's in Chicago because I only have a love seat and one chair in my living room. My mom is so short she can fit on the love seat just fine."

"Dalton's a puss about that stuff."

"Tell me about it."

I grab a towel to dry the dishes, our eyes locking for a second. When I'm standing this close to him, our height difference seems more pronounced. I've never been with a man as tall as him or as in shape.

He looks away and clears his throat. "I'm gonna head out."

I don't let my disappointment show. He's going in a different direction today in search of help. I'm feeling better and the swelling in my ankle has gone down, so the least I can do is stay here and pass the time while he hikes through two feet of snow trying to get us rescued.

"Do you want to take some food?" I ask.

He shakes his head. "I'll eat when I get back. Or when I run across a steak house."

I laugh at the thought. "Bring me back a loaded sweet potato if you find one."

When he smiles, the corners of his eyes crinkle in a way I find incredibly sexy. I've never reacted to a man just looking at me like I do when Lincoln does it. Somehow, he makes me want him with just a look that communicates in a way words can't.

"Are you okay with me going?" he asks.

I won't admit that I want him to stay. His going out in this weather to look for help is our only chance of rescue at this point. No search party will look for us inside this cabin. It's my anxiety that wants him here, safe inside the cabin with me.

"Of course. But be careful and turn around if the wind picks up."

"I will." He takes a step closer to me, the intensity of his gaze making my heart race with excitement. "I've got an idea for when I get back."

Sex. For the love of God, please let him say sweaty marathon sex. My face heats just from thinking about it.

"Oh?" My attempt at casual falls short, the word squeaking out of me.

I'm imagining how his beard will feel on my bare thighs when he says, "Boggle."

"Boggle?" My brows shoot up in surprise.

He nods toward a shelf near the kitchen table, which has the game of Boggle and a deck of cards on it. I don't let on how disappointed I am. Not that I really expected him to propose sex, but a girl can dream.

"Loser has to answer any question the winner asks," he says with a smug grin.

I take a step back to give my overworked heart a break from being so close to him. "Well, prepare for me to know all your dark secrets, then. I was an English major in college."

"I can take you."

"We'll see." I hang the towel on the bar mounted on a kitchen cabinet. "But best-case scenario, you come back with the entire Alaska National Guard to get us out of here."

The corners of his lips quirk up in a smile. "I'll do my best."

He holds my gaze for a couple of heart-pounding seconds before turning and walking over to the hooks by the front door, where his coat is hanging.

After bundling up, he puts a hand on the doorknob and looks back at me. "Don't worry about me, okay?"

I nod, giving him a confident and completely fake smile. Telling me not to worry while off of my anxiety meds is like telling the sun to stop shining.

EIGHTEEN HOURS LATER, I'M SWAYING TO THE sounds of Sinatra, my eyes squeezed shut as I fight my urge to throw open the cabin's front door and go searching for Linc.

He's been gone for too long. Every howl of the wind unnerves me as I imagine him out there in the snow. I should have told him I wanted him to stay here, where it's safe and warm. We have enough food to make it just fine until spring when the snowstorms will stop and the snow will start melting.

I wish I could talk to Genevieve. Even though we became friends because we're coworkers, we've become very close. We spend time together on weekends and holidays.

What would she say about all of this? Of course she'd say the whole thing is "fucking ridiculous" because she says that all the time. Then she'd get giddy over me being trapped in a cabin with one bed and a hot, single man.

Libidinous is too long of a word for Boggle, but it's absolutely me right now. I think about Lincoln day and night. My body has started to crave him. Normally I'm ninety-five percent logical, but he makes me feel ninety-five percent horny and maybe five percent logical.

Is it just the stress of this situation, or is there really a connection between us? As Frank serenades me from the record player with "New York, New York," I wonder who I'd choose to walk through that cabin door if I could be stuck here with anyone else.

Other than maybe an experienced helicopter pilot and a helicopter, I can't think of anyone.

Hell, who am I kidding? After the plane crash,

I'm never getting on anything that flies again, so even a helicopter pilot is out. I've been dreaming about the crash, and it's always the part where we're plunging to the ground, knowing we're going to hit it at any moment.

I exhale hard, putting thoughts of the crash out of my head. That won't help my anxiety.

What if Lincoln is close to the cabin and he just can't make it all the way back? I run over to the wall hooks and put on the flannel hanging there, then try to force my injured foot into one of my boots.

"Shit," I mutter because it hurts so badly.

But my foot fit into this boot when my ankle was more swollen than this, so I'll get it in there again. Holding my breath, I force my foot into the boot, then quickly get the other one on.

I open the door and walk outside the cabin for the first time since arriving here. Icy snow slaps me in the face.

The outdoor light illuminates the sparkling snow, where I can't see any footprints from when Linc left. I get dizzy, my pulse pounding frantically.

"Linc!" I race into the snow, looking in every direction. "Lincoln, can you hear me?"

There's not a single sound in response. Just the snow, which slowly trails from the sky, unbothered.

"Fuck!" I scream at the top of my lungs. "Linc, where are you?"

We're supposed to be eating rice and playing Boggle. I'm supposed to be flirting with him and feeling a thrill at the way his spine stiffens when I do.

I yell his name as loud as I can until my throat aches and I can't feel my soaking wet feet. It's not that I don't want to be alone in this cabin; it's the agony of thinking about what might have happened to him.

The way I feel after a long, intense bout with anxiety is like a hangover. I'm spent in every possible way as I drag myself back into the cabin and close the door behind me, pressing my back to it.

He's a good man. A really good one. I can't bear the thought of him freezing to death. All alone.

I kick off my boots and walk over to the fire, poking the logs to bring it back to life. If I'm going to be mentally strong, I have to push back against the worst-case scenarios my mind always ends up imagining.

Maybe he's been gone so long because he found help. Maybe he took shelter somewhere. I hope my friends and family haven't given up on me being alive, and when Lincoln's only been gone for—I look over at the clock—nearly nineteen hours, I won't give up on him.

I walk into the storage room and scan the contents of the shelves. I grab a few items, walk into the kitchen and set them on the counter.

Then I close my eyes, clear my mind, and set my palm on my chest below my breasts. I picture Linc, his hand on mine as he counts while I breathe.

I can't control so many things right now, so I focus on this—the only thing I have complete power over.

fourteen

LINCOLN

Everything looks the same. Snow and trees and more snow and trees. How the hell did I let myself get lost?

I stop walking and take a few deep breaths, measuring the depth of the snow by how far it comes up on my boots. It's close to the top and still snowing. At this rate, it'll be up to my knees soon.

If I let myself, I could go to sleep right here in the snow. It's only knowing I'd never wake up again that keeps me moving.

I have no idea how many hours I've been gone, but it's a lot. My exhaustion is bone deep. At some point, I crawled underneath a massive pine tree and rested for a couple of hours, but I didn't really sleep.

As I start trudging ahead again, I think about Trinity's Chicago apartment. Is she a neat freak, with everything in its proper place? Or would I find a few dishes in the sink and a chair in her bedroom layered with clothes?

I've been imagining sitting next to her on her love seat. My arm is around the back of it and she's close to me, giving me that playful smile that makes me wonder what she's thinking.

In this daydream, it's summer in Chicago, of course, and her apartment windows are open. It's a balmy eighty-five degrees and we're both sweaty. Her cat is perched on the arm of the love seat next to me. She laughs about how she was Karma's favorite person until I came along.

She has to be going out of her mind about why I haven't returned. If only I could text her and let her know I'm alive, trying to find my way back to the cabin.

Surprisingly, I don't miss my phone much. Well, other than my guilty pleasure, the AITA subreddit thread. They're *almost always* the asshole, and I love grabbing a bag of Doritos, getting comfortable in my recliner and taking a deep dive into the comments.

"Am I the asshole for wanting to ravage my best friend's sister?" I ask the empty icy landscape, short of breath from the exertion of walking through the deep snow. "She's beautiful, but it's more than just that. I can't even explain it, but I want to know everything there is to know about her. She's a lot younger than me and I should care more about that than I do."

I stop walking and squint when I see movement near the horizon. And fuck me if it's not a brown bear.

Shit. I really don't want to get attacked by a bear and have people discover it when they find my teeth in a pile of bear shit when the snow melts. That sounds like a worse death than freezing to death, though significantly quicker.

All the things that scared me before this experience were actually not even scary. I've always been scared I'd spend so long chasing hockey records that I'd retire past my prime, with people whispering that it was about damn time. I haven't had intercourse with a woman in more than a decade because it was always ruined by my worry I'd get her pregnant, which terrifies me. I don't want to have a kid with some woman I'm not married to and end up being an absentee dad who just sends money and shows up in my offseason to try and make up for all the time I missed.

I can see the headline: **Lincoln Rowe, digested by bear in Alaska, leaves behind a massive bank account and fuck all else.**

The bear disappears into the woods. I let out the breath I'm holding and start walking again. I have to keep my blood circulating, no matter how much I want to take a break. The few hours of sunlight for today will be over within an hour and I'll be back in the dark.

My mom always dreamed of visiting Alaska. She wanted to see glaciers. I could send her on as many Alaskan cruises as she wanted now, but she passed away before I went pro and started making great money.

Just thinking of her brings a lump to my throat. I got my work ethic from her and have lots of amazing memories, but her manipulation changed the course of my life. I don't want the power to ruin someone emotionally, and that's why I'm so dead set against having kids.

"You are definitely the asshole," I tell myself as I push forward, my legs burning with exertion.

"You're the asshole for wanting Trinity and for not bringing any food with you out here."

I'd tell any of my teammates in this situation to nut up and figure it out. I'm the levelheaded leader with absolutely no quit in me.

My voice of reason is starting to creep in, though, reminding me that I can't wander around in bitter cold indefinitely. I don't want to go out with a whimper, alone out here. But I may not get a choice.

The last of the day's sunlight fades away and I get my first wave of true panic. I'm breathing my way through it when I see a faint glow in the distance. I say a silent prayer.

If that's the cabin, I'll never ask for anything again. I won't ask to win hockey games or break records, I just want to live.

I pick up my pace, desperate to find out if it's the cabin light. The glow gets brighter. It has to be the cabin.

My victory yell sounds crazed. This is different than winning a game. This is my life, and there's still so much I want to do with it.

I make out the faint outline of the cabin and realize I'm approaching it from a completely different direction than the one I took when I left.

I'm damn lucky I found it. Without the light, I wouldn't have.

As I walk to final hundred yards, it also occurs to me that I wouldn't have made it without hockey. My legs are exceptionally strong from all the years of skating and conditioning.

When I get onto the porch, I dig the drifted snow away from the door with my hands, flinging it back between my legs. I'm not even finished when the door swings open.

I look up and see Trinity, her eyes brimming with tears though she's smiling wide.

"Get in here, you asshole! I've been worried sick about you."

I stand up and kick my way through the last foot of snow, stepping through the doorway. I pull my gloves off, my hands so cold I can't maneuver the zipper of my coat down.

Trinity reaches out and does it for me, sliding my coat off. It drops to the floor and she throws her arms around my neck. Closing my eyes, I wrap my arms around her waist and pull her close.

She's soft and warm, her curves molding against me. I can feel her crying into the crook of my neck so I tighten my hold on her.

"You can't get rid of me that easily," I quip.

I can hear the exhaustion in her laugh. She pulls back and cups my cheeks in her hands. "Are you okay?"

"Yeah, I'm okay."

Her expression relaxes. "Okay, let's get you warmed up and I'll get you some food."

She takes my arm and walks me over to the fireplace, where a fire is blazing. I sit down on the floor in front of it, the warmth like a soothing balm on my skin.

"How long was I gone?"

"Twenty-three hours." She puts the quilt from the bed around my shoulders. "I've been a mess. Don't go out there again, Linc. Please."

"I won't. I thought I was done for."

"What happened?" She looks back at me over her shoulder as she walks to the kitchen.

"I got lost. My tracks got covered by snow drifts. I came back from a totally different direction than the one I left in."

She shakes her head. "I'd rather just live here forever than risk you dying."

I consider her words as she pours me a cup of coffee. "Live here forever, huh? With a grouchy old hockey player?"

A smile plays on her lips as she brings the mug

over to me. "Maybe not. How old are you?"

"I'm 35."

"Oh, is that all? I thought you were at least forty-five." She gives me a playful look.

I scoot closer to the fire. "I saw a bear."

Her brows hit her hairline. "Are you serious? Was it aggressive?"

"No, it was way off in the distance. I don't think it even saw me. But I don't want to get any closer to one."

She nods. "I'm glad you're not going out again. I made food if you're hungry."

"I'm starving. What'd you make?"

"Taco soup and an apple crisp."

Now I'm the one giving her an incredulous look. "Apple crisp?"

"With dried apples. It turned out pretty well, but I don't have any ice cream to put on top of it."

My stomach growls painfully as I stand up. "I don't care. I'll take it and whatever taco soup is left."

She opens the cabinet to take out a bowl. I reach for the pot on the hotplate, taking it by the handle.

"No bowl?" she asks, puzzled.

I shake my head. "I'm eating it all, no reason to dirty another dish."

Amused, she passes me a spoon. I dig in immediately, closing my eyes as the first spicy bite touches my tastebuds.

"This is great."

She smiles and sits down across from me. "How much would you pay right now for an actual taco?"

"Hardshell or softshell?

She considers. "Hardshell. Warm, crunchy shell loaded with seasoned beef, queso, onions and tomatoes."

"Ten grand."

She bursts out laughing. "Are you serious?"

"Yep. I'd pay fifty grand for five of those. How much would you pay?"

"Well, I'm not a millionaire, but I'd do a few hundred." She passes me a big glass of water.

"Thanks." I drink half of it and set the glass back down. "How much for a huge banana split?"

"Oh." The word comes out of her mouth as a sensual moan. "A lot. Especially if it had caramel and strawberries and whipped cream."

"I'd go fifteen large for a banana split. And honestly, I wouldn't blink at twenty for a big, perfectly cooked filet mignon."

She hums her agreement. "See, that would be a major downside to staying here forever."

I'm looking at her longer than I should, and I notice the dark circles under her eyes. "Have you slept at all?"

"A couple of hours."

"We both need some sleep. I think we should pile on the covers and say fuck the fire until the cold wakes one of us up."

Amusement dances in her eyes. "Okay, fuck the fire."

I finish the pot of soup and then down the rest of the apple crisp, which turns out to be delicious.

"Keep your back to me while I change," Trinity says.

Two minutes later, she's wearing her long underwear. She puts the quilt back on the bed and then adds the afghan from the back of the couch. Every muscle from my waist down aches as I walk over to the bed, taking off my boots and socks.

"Is it okay if I take my jeans off? I promise--"

"Of course." She waves a hand dismissively.

"You don't even know what I was about to promise." Even dead on my feet, I couldn't resist a chance to make her blush.

Her laugh is nervous as she locks eyes with me. I

wink at her and her smile widens, but she looks away.

I slide out of the jeans, leaving me in boxers and a Henley. When I lie down on the firm flannel-sheet-topped mattress and pull the covers over myself, I groan with satisfaction.

Trinity turns off the lamp, stokes the fire one more time, and climbs into bed beside me.

"Are you warming up?" she asks.

My eyelids are heavy and I'm already fighting sleep. "Some. My feet are still numb."

I feel movement and the next thing I know, she's spooning me from behind. My eyes fly wide open with alarm. Her soft breasts are pressing against my back, and I don't mind it at all.

"Just warming you up," she says softly.

That's an understatement. The blood may not be flowing in my feet, but my cock is twitching to attention. This isn't me making a move on her, and it's not her making a move on me, either. But it feels damn good.

I'm too tired to overthink it, so I cover her hand with mine and give in to the pull of sleep.

fifteen

TRINITY

I'M FIGHTING MY URGE TO INHALE, KICKING MY LEGS wildly in a futile fight. It's dark. I claw at my scalp, trying to find the hands holding me beneath the water's surface, but I can't find them.

This is it. My chest burns, every impulse I have telling me this is the end of my life. A wave of panic seizes me. I reach out wildly, waving my arms in a desperate bid to make contact with anything.

My scream will be the end of me. It comes out silently, but I can still feel it deep inside.

"Trin?" Lincoln cries. "What the fuck is going on? Talk to me!"

I suck in a breath, my lungs filling with the oxygen I thought I'd never have access to again. I'm sitting up, my palms pressed to the mattress and my heart racing.

I'm in the cabin. It was the nightmare that has plagued me for years, and I must have actually screamed in real life and woken Lincoln up.

"I'm fine." I'm breathless, the anguish still fresh in my mind.

"Is there someone in here?"

I can tell from his voice that he's out of bed and close to the wall of weapons. That could go badly, so I force myself into a calmer state.

"I had a nightmare, Linc. I'm sorry I scared you."

His exhale is heavy with relief. "Fuck. The way you screamed, I thought--"

"I'm sorry."

I close my eyes, shame edging in to compete with my relief. Anxiety even follows me into sleep. Why am I like this? I just want to have normal dreams, like being able to fly.

"Hey." Lincoln's tone is soft, his voice closer to me now. "Nothing to be sorry for."

He gets back into bed and pulls the covers over himself.

"You're exhausted and I woke--" I stop talking as he pulls me into his arms, making sure my back stays covered by blankets.

"What was your nightmare about?" he asks.

I settle my cheek against his chest, his warm skin and strong embrace soothing me. He's not even a little bit irritated. My college boyfriend wouldn't stay the night with me because of my nightmares and the sleep they cost him.

"I was drowning."

"Damn. I've never had that one. My most frequent nightmare is that I shoot a goal for the other team and it wins them the game."

I smile, amused. "Where does that even come from?"

"Probably my unhealthy obsession with winning."

I've never snuggled against a man with a body like his. My palm rests on his chest, where I can feel his heart beating. My knee rests against his thigh and I think about hooking it over his leg, quickly dismissing the idea.

Just this. This comforting embrace is more contact than I've had with a man in a very long time, and it feels good. I don't want anything to ruin it.

"Where does the drowning nightmare come from?" he asks, his breath a warm caress on my forehead.

"Oh, um...I guess from my deep-seated anxiety?"

There's a moment of silence before he speaks again. "Is that something you're comfortable talking about, or should we talk about something else?"

"My anxiety?" His question catches me by surprise.

"Yeah."

"I don't mind talking about it."

"My teammate who had depression, his name was Jacques. And the thing he hated about it the most was that it would hit him out of nowhere sometimes. He'd say he had nothing to be depressed about, but it was there anyway. Is your anxiety like that?"

I hum softly against his chest, feeling seen. "Very much so. Anxiety is my baseline. I don't have to have a legitimate thing to worry about, but when I do have something big, it spirals. Or I guess it used to. The medication I'm on has been life-changing."

"When did you go on it?"

"In college. I was twenty-one and there was a campus therapist who told me about it."

He pulls me the tiniest bit closer and my pulse quickens. Am I just starved for human companionship, or are these feelings I'm having for him real?

"How's the withdrawal going?" he asks.

"Better. The sickness is a lot better, but...I don't know; it's just an adjustment. I forgot what it feels like to have anxiety at the forefront of my mind all the time."

"If there's ever anything I can do to help with it, let me know."

A wave of longing passes through me. My close friends and family who know about my anxiety aren't unsupportive, but they've never actually talked to me about it this way. And romantic partners have all been judgmental, wanting to know why I was anxious and how to fix it.

Lincoln seems to accept that it's just part of who I am.

"Thanks," I murmur. "Do you have any weaknesses?"

He laughs lightly. "Hell yes I do."

A few moments of quiet pass while I wait for him to elaborate.

He sighs softly. "I like to be in control. I hold on

to grudges for too long. And I eat too many Reese's cups."

I laugh and slide my palm over his chest, tilting my face toward him. "Reese's cups?"

"They're my crack. I could take down an entire bag at once."

"Well, hockey players need a lot of calories."

"Tell my trainers that. The older I get, the harder it is to keep weight off."

I furrow my brow. "You have to worry about that?"

"Yeah. Your brother has a freakish metabolism and can eat anything he wants, but I have to eat pretty clean. Extra pounds slow me down."

I yawn, sleepiness tugging my eyes closed. "Don't you think it should be colder in here?"

It's cold, but not ice cold, like it should be with the fire out.

"This place seems to be well insulated."

I want to stay awake and keep enjoying this, but his warmth is lulling me back to sleep. The last thing I feel is him tightening his hold on me slightly, keeping me close.

SEVERAL HOURS LATER, LINCOLN WALKS BACK INTO the cabin with water to fill the tub when I burst out of the storage room.

"If I told you I just found the most amazing thing possible in the storage room, what would you think it is?"

"Uh..." He lowers his brows, the wrinkle between them appearing. "A breakfast buffet with bacon and eggs?"

"No, better. This is something that will last longer than one meal." I hold up my hand with my find. "Toothbrushes! And toothpaste!"

"Hell yeah."

"I'm going to brush for five full minutes. There's a big metal box of toiletries in there."

I don't mention that it has tampons, pads and condoms—so many condoms—because that feels awkward.

Lincoln was busy making oatmeal in the kitchen when I woke up earlier. I was hoping to wake up first and enjoy some more time snuggled up to him, but no such luck. And in the few hours we've been up, neither of us has said anything about it.

As I watch him pouring a bucket of water into the tub, I wonder what he'd say if I told him he doesn't have to look away when I undress this time.

I almost burst out laughing. He'd flip his shit. Lincoln is a gentleman. And while I find that attractive, I find my mind wandering to thoughts of him *not* being a gentleman.

We've started dipping into the drinking water supply in the storage room, deciding we can refill the containers with snow when they're empty. I pour myself a glass of water and use it to brush my teeth, and I don't take the clean feeling for granted.

Lincoln takes a break from the water to brush his teeth, too, and I hold back a joke that's not really a joke about us kissing to test out our fresh breath.

"Want some help filling the tub?" I offer instead.

"Nope. I've got it."

"You go first this time."

He lifts a corner of his lips in a smile. "You're not using my dirty bathwater, Trin. You go first."

I hold his gaze for a few seconds, replaying the sound of him calling me *Trin* and liking it. A lot. In less than a month, I've gone from being annoyed by him to wanting him to ravage me.

He said he'd help with my anxiety however he could, and orgasms are scientifically proven to be relaxing.

Imagining his powerful body on top of me sends a shot of arousal coursing through me. He's dead sexy in the looks department, but it's everything else about him that has me wanting him so badly I can't think about anything else.

What busted up ankle? What anxiety? All I can think about is how he looks and sounds when he comes.

"All ready for you," he announces.

He finished filling the tub while I imagined him doing every X-rated thing I could come up with. I'm over admonishing myself about it. We're two single, consenting adults alone in a cabin with one bed. What better way to pass the time than getting lost in each other?

I get a towel and clean clothes, my heart hammering as I build up my confidence to make the first move. He's too much of a gentleman; it has to be me.

When I reach for the top button on the oversized flannel I'm wearing, he quickly turns his back.

"Turn back around," I say, light-headed from nervousness.

I can do this. I've seen him looking at me. We both want it.

He looks over his shoulder. "Everything okay?"

My hands are working quickly now, and soon I'm down to the fourth button, cool air brushing over my skin where the shirt hangs open. Linc quickly turns his head away from me again.

"It's okay to look," I assure him. "I...I want you to."

His shoulders sink. "Fuck."

That wasn't the reaction I was expecting. Shame floods me as I pull the shirt closed again.

"It's not that I don't want you," he says. "I think you're beautiful and I want you more than you know. But..."

"It's okay. You don't have to explain."

My skin is hot with embarrassment from my forehead to my toes. What was I thinking? Now every minute we spend together will be awkward.

"It's Dalton."

I furrow my brow. "My brother? Oh God. Are you guys...together?"

"Jesus, Trin. No. But he's my best friend. He's like a brother to me. He asked me to keep you safe, and I...don't want to take advantage of this situation."

This is so humiliating. Even when I'm the only

woman for—how many miles? Hundreds?—he still doesn't want me.

"It's okay. You don't need to explain."

I allow myself to look at his back, which is tight with tension.

"I want to look. I want...hell, I want to do a lot more than look. But--"

"Stop talking!" My words come out harsher than I intended. "Please. Let's pretend this never happened."

His shoulders sink with a sigh. I scramble out of my clothes and into the tub, where no amount of scrubbing washes away my complete and total embarrassment over his rejection.

The one time I didn't overthink something and let anxiety protect me from being hurt. I won't let that happen again.

sixteen

LINCOLN

WHY DID I SAY *FUCK*? OF ALL THE THINGS THAT could have come out of my mouth when Trinity said I could watch her undress, I said *fuck*, and I can't stop replaying it in my head.

It's been almost twenty-four hours since that exchange. I didn't mean it the way she took it, but I know she doesn't want to hear my explanation.

She's been rereading a book since she woke up this morning, playing records and refusing to even make eye contact with me. Michael Bublé is currently singing about how good he's feeling, a stark contrast to the tense mood in the cabin.

"Trin."

She glances up from her book, brows raised. "What's up?"

"I didn't mean it like you took it. When I said *fuck*—"

"We agreed to pretend that never happened." She slams the book closed and stands up from the love seat. "I'm going outside."

"Outside?"

She walks over to the wall hooks where my coat and hat are hanging. "I just need some fresh air. I'm going stir-crazy in here."

I shake my head. "That's--"

She cuts me off again. "I'm not asking for permission. I'm going to stay close to the cabin."

I walk over to the front door and open it to look outside. It's snowing so hard I can't see anything but the dense mass of falling flakes.

"Not now." I close the door decisively. "At least wait until it quits snowing."

She smiles, but not at me. "I can survive snowfall."

Fucking agitating woman. I grab one of my boots and pull it on. At least there's enough snow gear here for us to both be covered, but this is insane.

"Look, I get that you want to get out of here because things are tense," I start.

She meets my gaze, the fire in her eyes making me forget the rest of what I was about to say. "I'm going outside *alone*."

"No, you're not."

She throws her arms up. "Stop treating me like a child. I know how to take care of myself and cope with my anxiety."

"This is about your anxiety? Is it because of last night?"

When she narrows her eyes, I can practically feel the waves of disgusted anger rolling off of her.

"I have anxiety twenty-four seven. Believe it or not, not everything is about you."

I take a step closer to her and her eyes flare slightly. "You know how easy it would be for me to jump into bed with you? You don't think that's what the caveman in me wants more than anything?"

She scoffs. "So you're saying you happen to find the only woman within a hundred-mile radius attractive now that you've been stuck with me for weeks and there are no other options?"

I run a hand through my hair, my single note of laughter more frustrated than amused. "You think I rejected you last night, but I fucking didn't. I rejected taking advantage of you."

With only a couple feet of space between us, she holds her ground, her chin tilted up so our gazes stay locked. "Because I'm just a kid, right? Dalton's twenty-six-year-old kid sister."

"It's not about your fucking age. You don't fuck your teammate's wives or sisters. That's sacred. And even if I could get past that, how could I be sure you truly wanted it and it had nothing to do with your anxiety?"

Her chin drops and her eyes widen. "What the fuck? What could this possibly have to do with my anxiety?"

"Like I said, I know more about depression than anxiety, but I know self-soothing is a thing. Coping with alcohol or drugs or sex. My teammate went through that."

Her shoulders slump with defeat. "That's not me. Whether you believe me or not, I had to *overcome* my anxiety to say what I did last night. It's the opposite of self-soothing."

Fuck. She's killing me. I step closer to her, cupping her face in my hands. "It's not that I didn't want you. I did. *I do.* But Trin...I'm fucked up. If you really knew me, you wouldn't want me anymore."

Sadness swims in her eyes. "You have so many excuses. And that's all they are. You don't need to spare my feelings."

"I swear to you, every single reason that feels like an excuse to you is real to me. I care about you, and I don't fuck women I care about."

She pushes her brows together. "That makes no sense."

I shrug. "I meant it when I said I'm fucked up."

"So you only like casual sex? One-night stands?"

Part of me wants to be completely honest with her. Tell her things I've never shared with anyone. Instead, I give her a slice of the truth and nothing more.

"I don't even do that."

Then I lean down and brush my lips over hers, forcing myself to keep my hands on her face instead of letting them roam all the places I'm dying to explore. She lets out a small moan of surprise but then sinks into me. The kiss I intended to be short and sweet turns into much more as she parts her lips and my hunger for her comes pouring out.

She even tastes sweet. I knew she would. I slide

one of my hands down to her neck, then around to cup the back of her neck as I back her against the wall of the cabin. Her hands clutch my back with so much certainty I almost say fuck it and drop to my knees to unfasten her pants.

Just a kiss. That's all this can be. One kiss to show her how fucking much I want her.

My erection grinds into her stomach and she pulls away from the kiss, gasping for air. Her arms remain locked around me as I lean my forehead against hers, not ready to break our contact yet.

"Stay inside," I say against her lips. "I have a better idea than running around in a snowstorm."

"Oh, really?"

I groan. "It's not that. I wish like hell it was, but it's something else. Something fun."

I can feel her smiling. "Fun sounds good."

"Truth."

Trinity announces her choice and downs a shot of vintage Macallan whiskey. I saw the unopened bottle stashed in the storage room a few days ago and decided to use it to up the stakes in our first game of Boggle.

Truth or Dare Boggle is simple, really: you lose, you have to pick a truth or a dare and down a shot of whiskey. Considering each game only lasts three minutes, we're on a fast track to getting wasted.

"How did you lose your virginity?" I ask.

Her smile is shy. "I lost it to my college boyfriend, Dallas."

"Dallas?" I scoff.

"He was a virgin, too. It lasted less than a minute."

We lock eyes and both burst out laughing. That must have been comical.

"He didn't reciprocate or anything?" I ask.

She shrugs. "He tried, but...I was so uncomfortable. It's kind of impossible for me to relax when I'm with someone for the first time. I've only been with one other man, and it took more than a month for me to relax enough that I wanted to get on top and get myself off."

I just stare for a few seconds, dumbfounded. "Wait. You had to get yourself off? He couldn't do it?"

"I mean...he tried. I'm just so uptight that he couldn't. And it was fine. I figured out how being on top works."

Christ. I'm completely hard. Again. Knowing

Trin's never been with a real man who took the time to get her off—repeatedly—makes it even harder for me to stay on my side of the kitchen table.

"Did he eat your pussy?"

Her cheeks flush. "No, I'm too self-conscious for that."

She wouldn't be with me. I'd take as much time as I needed so she was comfortable and into it. But since I'm actively trying *not* to end up in bed with her, I force myself to move on.

I lose the next game of Boggle, the whiskey going down smoothly. Pretty sure reimbursing the cabin owner for that bottle is going to cost me a pretty penny, but I don't give a fuck. Trinity and I both need to unwind and have some fun.

"Truth," I proclaim, plunking the shot glass onto the table.

She's ready. Her lips curve into a sexy smile as she asks, "How many times have you masturbated since we've been here?"

"Uh..." I grin at her and clear my throat. "Three times."

Her eyes widen in surprise. "Three? That's it?"

I laugh. "What, are you flicking the bean every day in the outhouse or something?"

Her eyes dance playfully. "You have to win a game if you want me to answer that."

She shakes up the letters in the Boggle cube to start the next game. Both of us spend the first minute furiously writing down words, but after that, I can only concentrate on thoughts of Trinity never being fucked to orgasm by a man. She might as well just use a vibe if she has to be on top every time to get off.

By the end of the three minutes, her list is so much longer that I just shake my head.

"You whipped my ass," I mutter.

She pours a shot and passes me the glass. "Bottoms up, captain."

Bottoms up. *Fuck.* Now I'm imagining her round, gorgeous ass in the air. This is heaven and hell, the lines so blurred I can't remember a single reason why I shouldn't pick her up and carry her over to the bed right now.

I tip back the shot, a comfortable buzz making me relaxed. Trinity looks at me intently from the other side of the table.

"When you said you don't even have casual sex, what did you mean?"

I freeze. Why did I tell her that? Her eyes stay

locked onto me as I rub a hand over my short beard, considering what to say.

"All the things you could dare me to do and you'd rather ask me that?"

She nods.

I exhale heavily. That's something I never talk about, to anyone. But the whiskey and this cabin that feels like it's on the edge of the world make me care less. She bared her soul to me about her anxiety—I might as well be honest with her, too.

"I haven't had intercourse with a woman in—" I stop to do the math. "I'm thirty-four now, so I guess it's been nine years."

Her jaw drops with surprise. "Why?"

"I'm...too worried I'll get a woman pregnant. I usually couldn't even come from sex because I was so worried about it." A few seconds of silence pass before I continue. "Oral and anal can be just as good, you know."

Saying it makes me feel exposed. It's so much more comfortable for everyone to think I'm a red-blooded man who fucks every willing single woman I encounter.

Trinity clears her throat. "Are you just saying that to make me feel better about you not wanting to fuck *me*?"

I laugh a single note. "Uh, no. It's the truth."

"And women are okay with it?"

"You'd be surprised how much women enjoy having their pussies eaten and being finger fucked until they're squirting all over the bed."

Her cheeks turn pink and I can actually see the bob in her throat when she swallows. I can already see us both ending up on the floor from this variation of the game of Boggle.

The hangover tomorrow will be so fucking worth it.

seventeen

TRINITY

My head is made of concrete. I let it fall back onto the pillow immediately, groaning from the pounding sensation.

I had a lot of whiskey last night. Though I'm hurting right now, I also feel lighter. Linc and I laughed more than we have in our entire time here. We shared a lot. We both leaned into a free fall, not worrying about how hard we might hit at the end.

We both chose all truths in our game, learning each other's secrets and laughing about our embarrassments. I thought I might pee my pants from laughing when he told me his story of getting an erection in front of his entire class in seventh grade because he was hot for his teacher. And now he knows I mispronounced Lena Horne's last name in a speech in front of my entire middle school, humiliating myself.

Though I don't want to move, I need water. When I sit up and look around the cabin, I don't see Linc anywhere. My heart flutters with worry as I slide out of bed.

The bottle of whiskey is still on the kitchen table, about a quarter of it left. There's a note next to it.

Outside exercising. Be back soon.

L

I smile at the message, which feels almost intimate. After last night, I have a better understanding of Linc. There are still so many questions I want to ask him, but I'm not sure my body can handle more *Truth or Dare Boggle* just yet.

I drink a glass of water, refill it and drink half of the second glass. Today needs to be about rest and hydration for me.

My ankle is much better and letting loose last night helped my anxiety. If it wasn't winter, Lincoln and I would probably pack up supplies and start hiking, but we can't risk hitting a snowstorm.

I wonder if my office has been cleaned out. Has someone been hired to replace me at work? When I do eventually make it back home, will I still have a job?

Even with a hangover, questions still fly through my mind at a rapid-fire pace. I want to go back home—very much. But I don't hate it here. Not at all. There are no alarm clocks or schedules. I've never spent so much time just *being*, reading books and listening to music.

Life can't be like this all the time, but the break from sixty-hour workweeks has been nice.

I start making the oatmeal we eat for breakfast every day, fantasizing about having a plate of hot, crispy bacon to go with it. And *oh my god*, fresh-squeezed orange juice. Just thinking about the sweet juice and the salty bacon makes my mouth water.

It'll be nice to get back to the land of grocery stores and restaurants, but for now, I'm grateful for what we do have. This cabin and its food store saved our lives.

Lincoln opens the front door, a gust of icy air sending snowflakes in with him.

"Hey, morning." He takes off his coat and hangs it up.

"Morning."

Why does it feel like we slept together last night? I focus on my oatmeal prep, knowing I'm going to blush the first time our eyes meet. Our kiss and all the secrets we shared left me with a floaty, dreamy feeling that only gets stronger now that he's back in the cabin with me.

"Want some oatmeal?" I ask lightly.

"Yeah, that sounds great."

"How much snow did we get?"

"Uh...a foot, maybe?" He groans with satisfaction after pulling off a snow boot. "I made snowshoes. That's a fucking workout, walking through thirty inches of snow in those things."

"Well, you're a man, so it's probably more like eighteen inches."

"You've got the jokes!" I smile as his deep voice gets closer to me. "Will you be here all week?"

I shrug. "Depends how good the audience is."

I feel him standing behind me and I'm about to turn around and get the uncomfortable eye-contact blush out of the way when he wraps his arms around me from behind.

My lips part. It feels amazing, having his big, carved body against my back. I set down the oatmeal spoon and lean back against him. His arms are banded around me beneath my breasts and the cold seeps from him to me, but it doesn't bother me at all.

"I'm sweaty," he says apologetically.

"It's okay."

It really, *really* feels like we slept together last night. This is the morning-after cuddle session.

"How you feeling?" he asks, his warm breath near my ear giving me goose bumps.

"Like death."

He chuckles. "Yeah, I'm hurting too. It was fun, though."

"You want a rematch later?"

"You might want to check in with your liver and see if you're still up for it."

I laugh. "Maybe we'll need to modify the rules."

"I'm down. I'll have to move around a few things on my schedule, of course."

"Of course. My day is packed, too."

"Could you pencil in a little time after we eat for some dancing?"

My heart races with excitement. "Dancing?"

He steps back and I immediately miss his closeness. Leaning a hip on the kitchen counter, he looks down at me. "I know you want to grind all over me while we dance to some Sinatra."

I laugh hard at that. "So much."

His expression turns serious. "You're beautiful."

My heart stutters as I lock eyes with him. "I bet you say that to all the women you've survived plane crashes with."

The corners of his lips turn up in a soft smile. "Don't deflect, Trin. You're beautiful. You make me wish I could be...different."

"Different?"

He looks away and clears his throat. "Better."

I wonder if he's talking about his hang-up about sex. Because if there's something I understand very well, it's feeling like you're not right for most people. Too much. I know exactly how it feels to look like you have it all together on the outside when, inside, you're falling apart.

"I wouldn't change a thing about you," I say softly.

I stir the oatmeal, which is close to boiling over, and he pushes away from the counter, the moment over.

Hopefully he'll think about what I said. My

attraction to him has grown so much deeper over the past day now that I know more about him.

I understand him in a way I can't even put into words.

An hour later, we've finished breakfast and filled our empty five-gallon job with snow. Lincoln tended the fire and put an Etta James album on a few minutes ago, and he's standing in the open floor space by the record player waiting for me.

I used a washcloth to clean myself up and changed into a clean flannel, but I'm missing my toiletries pretty hard right now. I want makeup and perfume. My many flat irons and curling irons. My deliciously scented coconut lotion.

"Come on," Linc says. "Don't be nervous."

"Oh, I'm..."

His gaze locks onto mine and I don't even bother finishing the sentence. Because yeah, I'm nervous. Even my laugh sounds uptight.

"Is it weird that I was okay getting naked for you, but I'm nervous about dancing with you?"

His lips quirk into a smile. "Would you feel more comfortable getting naked to dance?"

My laugh is genuine this time. "No, I'm good."

He puts a hand out and my heart hammers harder. How is he so damn sweet? I've never known a man who didn't do everything in his power to get me into bed as quickly as possible if he thought he had a chance at it.

I take the few steps separating us and put my hand in his. He laces our fingers together and wraps his free arm around my waist, pulling me close. I rest my head against his shoulder and put my arm around his back.

We sway in silence for a couple of songs. Then "At Last" starts playing, and he releases my hand and puts his other arm around me, holding me close against him. I wrap my other arm around his back, one hand on his neck. I slide my fingers into his hair.

He's hard, and a delicious thrill passes through me. Whether he lets himself do anything more than this with me, I at least know he wants me. And I want him back so much it's an ache inside me.

I feel him sliding the back of my shirt up, moving it until he can put his arms around my bare skin. The feel of his touch on my lower back makes me exhale a sigh.

A log falls and crackles sound from the fireplace.

It's not really even warm in here, but I'm warm from head to toe from being this close to Lincoln.

"How many times have you been in love?" he asks me softly.

"Mmm...once, I guess."

"With the college guy?"

"No, the guy I dated after college. It lasted a year."

"You over him?"

I laugh softly. "Yes. I was the one who ended things."

"Why?"

"It just ran its course, I guess. He started drinking more and I found an open browser on my computer where he'd been looking at porn. I just felt it deep inside, you know? That he wasn't the one."

"Yeah."

"What about you? How many times have you been in love?"

More than thirty seconds pass before he finally answers. "Never. I told you I'm fucked up."

"Why is that fucked up?"

He sighs softly. "I guess it's more the reason that's fucked up. I'm so hung up on what happened to my parents. And to me, when they got divorced, that I'm never letting it happen to me."

My heart cracks as I think about how lonely that must be.

"Is it that you don't trust anyone or that you don't trust yourself?" I ask.

"Both."

There are so many things I want to say, but I stop myself. He didn't choose to feel this way; no one wants to be different from everyone around them. Isolated. Just like I didn't choose anxiety.

"I get what it's like to have something happen that changes you," I say.

He slides a hand down and cups my ass, a smile in his voice as he asks, "You like being spanked?"

Arousal floods me hard. My head is saying no, but every other body part is saying *hell yes, please now*.

"I don't...um, no one's ever done it."

I feel his hum in my chest. "Who are these shitty guys you've been with, Trin? They don't eat your pussy 'til you see stars, they don't spank you when you've been a bad girl and they don't fuck you well."

Rest in Peace, ovaries.

"You don't do any of those things, either," I remind him. "Unfortunately."

He groans and slides a hand down the back of my leggings, squeezing my bare ass. I gasp.

"It's about time we change some of that," he says in my ear, his voice gruff. "I can't give you everything, but...we can play. Is that enough?"

My pulse pounds and my head swims as I manage a strangled, "Yes."

eighteen

LINCOLN

I can only see Trinity's outline in the faint light of the flickering fire, but I can feel her heart beating steadily against my chest as we lie down on the bed.

On the way to the bed, I unbuttoned her shirt and slid it to the floor, then added mine to the floor right after. I can't get enough of her bare skin against mine. Her breath on my cheek. Her hair brushing against my chest.

I don't know if it's because we survived a plane crash together and fought our way through brutal cold to make it to the cabin, but there's a bond between us now. I've felt the bond tightening faster and faster, literally pulling us together. I can't think only of Dalton anymore. This connection is something Trinity and I both need.

I won't sleep with her. That'll have to be enough for Dalton when we see each other again. Right now, there's only one other person in my world, and I can't keep her at arm's length any longer.

"What's this?" Trinity murmurs as she runs her fingers over a small raised scar on my shoulder blade.

"Got grazed by a knife when I was breaking up a bar fight a couple years ago." She gasps and I hum with amusement. "It's nothing. I've been cut worse playing hockey."

I kiss my way down her chest and she wraps her legs around my waist. My cock throbs with need. I've done this with women many times, but there's something different about Trinity. It's like my soul has known hers for a very long time and we've finally reconnected after being apart.

When I move onto my back, I take her hips and move her on top of me. She exhales hard when she feels my erection against her, shifting her hips just enough to make me groan.

She's so beautiful, her hair loose around her shoulders. I find her even more beautiful now that I know her better. She's strong, though it doesn't come naturally to her. Her strength is something she's fighting for every day here, grappling not only with the unknowns of our situation but her anxiety, too.

I sit up slightly and reach for the clasp of her bra, but she uses both hands and pulls it up over her head, tossing it aside.

My hands find her breasts in the near darkness, her gasp sending a shudder through me. This is about her, but my body doesn't seem to get it. I'm trembling inside like a high school kid with a crush.

When I lightly pinch her nipples, she grinds against me, making me close my eyes and force myself to gain control. I'm not going to come in my pants—or at all—but she's going to make it one hell of a fight.

"Don't move your hips," I tell her as I cup her breasts and squeeze them gently. "Be completely still."

"Completely?" She arches her back, slightly increasing the pressure against my cock.

I take her hips and move her off of me, then sit

up. "You're not much at following instructions, sexy girl."

"*Girl?*" She sounds both offended and turned on.

"That's right. You're an inexperienced girl who's never been with a real man. You're going to lie over my lap and do exactly as I say."

She complies immediately, lying over me as I sit on the edge of the bed with my feet on the floor. I rub my palm over her ass and squeeze each cheek, then use both hands to pull her leggings down until they're just above her knees.

"Do you want them off?" she asks breathlessly.

I answer with a hard smack against her ass, making her inhale sharply. "If I wanted them off, I'd take them off. This way, you're forced to keep your legs closed. You'd spread them wide open if I let you, wouldn't you?"

There's a pause and then a whispered, "Yes."

I squeeze each of her ass cheeks again, then smack her harder. "Jesus fuck, this ass. Just begging to be spanked. And you fucking like it, don't you?"

"Yes."

She squirms a little and I respond immediately. "You aren't trying to rub your pussy against my leg, are you?"

She's silent and I spank her again. This time, she tries to hold back a moan. I take one side of her panties and move them into the crack of her ass, then do the same with the other side. I spank one bare ass cheek and then tug on the panties in the crack of her ass so they rub against her clit in the front.

"*Oh.*"

I tug again, holding on to her panties as she muffles her moan with a blanket. I can tell she wants to move her hips, but she stays still.

My cock continues throbbing beneath her as I tug on her panties and loosen my hold, giving her just enough friction to want more.

"That feels good." It's almost a whimper, and it feeds my hunger for her.

I release her panties and smack her ass again, rubbing my palm over it right after to soothe the sting. Then I slide my fingers inside her panties and into her slick pussy, and I feel her body stiffen slightly.

"No nerves with me, sexy girl," I say in a low tone. "Just relax and let me drive. You can feel what you do to me, can't you?"

She moans her agreement, drawing her knees up slightly to give me greater access. I stroke the folds of her pussy with my middle finger and she gasps sharply when I reach her clit.

I groan, my erection pulsing hard. "So swollen and wet."

When I circle her clit with the pad of my finger, her answering moan is long and needy. "Linc...god that feels...oh *please*."

I keep circling, and it doesn't take long for her body to tense as she cries out. The pulse of her orgasm sends a shot of satisfaction through me. She circles her hips, riding out the satisfaction. When she drops down with an exhale, I move my hand and slide out from beneath her.

We both move until we're lying side by side on the bed, facing each other.

"I can't believe that just happened," she murmurs. "I've never come the first time I was with someone."

"It wasn't you; it was them," I assure her.

"I've also never..." Her voice trails off.

My curiosity is too piqued to let that slide. "Never what?"

When she doesn't respond, I prod her playfully. "Don't make me bring Boggle over here."

She laughs softly. "I've never had anyone touch me other than...me."

It takes me a few seconds to process that. "So you've never had anything but straight-up sex?"

She hums with amusement. "Ironic, isn't it? That the only thing I've ever done is the only thing you don't do."

"That just means I have lots of things to introduce you to."

She snuggles closer to me. "Don't tell me how many asses you've spanked to get so good at this."

"Not as many as you probably think."

"Just because you don't want to?"

"Because I don't have sex. I don't like having to explain myself and it's not something I want everyone knowing."

She smoothes a hand over my cheek. "I won't tell a soul. I swear it."

"I know. I trust you."

"I get how it feels to not trust birth control completely. That's Anxiety 101—always assume the worst will happen."

I sigh softly. "Part of me wishes I wasn't like this. But my greatest fear is getting a woman pregnant. That's just how it is."

She kisses my forehead. "Never be ashamed of who you are. I happen to think you're pretty great just as you are."

The bond between us tugs tighter. No woman but Trinity has ever accepted that I didn't want to have sex. I've been laughed at, yelled at and called a head case over it.

"What's your greatest fear?" I ask.

Her answer is immediate. "Drowning."

I remember the panic in her scream when she woke up in a sweat. "Like in your nightmare."

"Yes."

I lie on my back and put my arm out, pulling her against me. She snuggles into my side and I cover us both up. "Does that come from something that happened to you?"

Her exhale is soft and warm on my chest. "When I was fourteen, I was swimming at a lake in a friend's neighborhood. We were on a dock in the middle of the lake when this sixteen-year-old guy who loved making fun of me showed up. Joey Marconi. He pushed me into the lake and held my head under the water."

I can tell from the emotion in her voice that this wound is still fresh for her.

"Jesus, Trin. That's fucking awful."

"I was already panicked from being pushed in, and I hadn't taken a breath before he pulled me under, so I inhaled a bunch of water. I can't even describe how scared I was. He was so strong, and I...I really thought I was going to die."

"That would be terrifying for anyone. I'm sorry that happened."

She sighs softly. "I haven't been swimming since that day."

"Could I get you into a hot tub if we had one?"

"Oh, definitely. Can you even imagine?"

I picture it. Me and Trin in a hot tub in the cabin, sipping on drinks and watching snow fall through the window. We're both naked, of course. It's my idea of heaven.

She puts her arm around my chest and gives me a little squeeze. "I know I was a pain in the ass when we first crashed and got here, but I'd choose you, Linc. To be stuck here with."

"I'd choose you, too."

Pushing up on her elbow, she leans over me and kisses me. My cock was already hard just from having her next to me, and the kiss makes it strain against my pants.

I cup her face with one hand and squeeze her ass with the other. She nips lightly on my lower lip as she slides a hand over my crotch, cupping my erection.

"Oh, fuck." I groan and put my hand over hers.

"Let me," she says against my lips.

"I don't...I just wanted this to be about you."

She rubs her palm over my cock, making me groan again. "Nothing is just about you or me here. It's always *us*."

I don't know if it's her logic or how fucking good it feels to have her touching me, but I relent and move my hand away.

"No sex," she murmurs. "I'd never do that to you."

It's been a long time since a woman touched me. I close my eyes and exhale long and hard as she unfastens my jeans and pulls them down. When she bends to kiss my cock through my underwear, a shudder passes through me. I never do this—give up control to a woman in bed. I satisfy them in every way I can, and if I allow myself anything, I'll let them suck me for a little while, but I always finish myself.

But Trin gave herself over to me just now. She trusts me, and I trust her.

She tugs my underwear off and licks the head of my cock, making my breathing ragged. When she takes me in her mouth, I fist the quilt on the bed, fighting to keep control.

Her soft hair brushes over my thighs as she takes

me deeper. It's so fucking good. So much different than with a random woman I met in a bar.

I'm not going to last long. I lean up on one elbow. "Hey, come here. Touch me. I want you up here where I can kiss you."

She does, lying on her side right next to me. Her soft hand strokes my hard, wet cock and I groan.

I brush the hair back from her face, the fire putting out just enough light for me to see her outline and know her eyes are locked onto mine.

It's been so long, and the intensity of Trin being the one touching me has amplified everything to a point that I can't hold on. When her soft kiss turns into a deeper one, I groan into her mouth as I come hard and long.

She keeps stroking me until the wave crests, satisfaction making my whole body go slack. I kiss her, feeling something I can't wrap my head around.

"Thank you," I say softly.

"Thank you for letting me."

I get out of bed to add a log to the fire, clean myself up and start a new record. I bring Trin a washcloth to clean herself up and then we snuggle under the covers.

My mind is clear and at peace, which is rare with so many unanswered questions from being stranded here. Hopefully after tonight, Trin will agree with me that Boggle is the second-best thing to do for fun here.

nineteen

SIX WEEKS LATER

TRINITY

I SNOWSHOE BACK TO LINCOLN AS FAST AS I CAN— which is not very fast, honestly. Snowshoes are bulky and there's still two feet of snow on the ground.

"We got a rabbit!" I hold up the animal my snare caught, grinning like I just won a coveted prize.

Linc's wide smile makes my heart race even faster. "My mouth's watering already. We're having meat for dinner tonight!" He pumps his fist. "Great job, gorgeous."

I soak up his praise like a dried-out sponge. It has to show on my face. Surely actual hearts appear in my eyes when he calls me *gorgeous*. And when he praises me in bed? My body doesn't just hum; it sings like a Southern gospel choir—loud, unapologetic and crying out my thanks to all that is holy.

"Here, I'll put it on the porch." Linc reaches for the rabbit. "We've got snow sprints to do."

It takes all my energy to keep smiling because *snow sprints*. When the snow storms calmed down around three weeks ago, Linc developed a daily outdoor workout plan for us. He said it would help him return to the ice immediately when we get out of here, and it's also been good for my anxiety.

If you define "good" as exhausting me to the point that I fall asleep quickly because my body is too worked out to worry, that is.

"Let's up it to five down and backs today," he says when he snowshoes back over to me.

I scoff. A "down and back" consists of us snowshoeing all the way across the long clearing in front of the cabin and back to the edge of the woods. And Linc doesn't just want us to do it—he wants us to do it *quickly*.

"You do remember that the only exercise I got before ending up here was walking from my office to the train station or Starbucks?"

"You've reminded me at least eighty times. You're getting better at this every day."

I force a smile. Considering I fell twice and ended up wheezing on day one, it really wasn't hard to get better.

"Come on." He leads the way. "Your heart will thank you."

"My butt muscles may pull a switchblade on my heart, though. Just sayin'."

He arches a brow, a grin playing on his lips. "You're pretty sassy for a woman who was woken up with two orgasms and breakfast in bed."

That's not an unusual way for me to wake up these days, and it definitely helps soften the downsides to being here, like running out of coffee two weeks ago.

"I'll do my best," I promise. "It's good that you know CPR."

He rolls his eyes. "You're not gonna die, Trin."

We start our first snow sprint, my breath making a cloud in front of me. It's cold, but when we're bundled up, it's no longer so cold it's painful to be out here. My ankle is completely healed. I think Lincoln's trying to build up my stamina so when spring comes, we can consider packing up supplies and hiking to civilization.

It's been more than two months since our plane crashed. This remote cabin seems like a place where very little changes, but that hasn't been true for me.

I still think about work sometimes, but it's no longer with a sense of panic that all my years of hard work were for nothing. I'm here and work is there, and I can't change that.

My anxiety is still there, but I'm coping with it. Linc meditates with me every morning, and our workouts are helping a lot, though I haven't admitted that to him. We don't have unlimited food here, but since we've been supplementing it by hunting small game with snares, I don't stress about running out. Now that I can walk and we have plenty of supplies, I'm confident we can make it out of here when the weather clears enough.

The biggest change of all has been between me and Linc, though. We've become closer than I've ever been to anyone, and I've left all my sexual insecurities behind.

It turns out I *can* strip down and straddle a hot man's face in broad daylight, and it's fucking incredible. It's ironic that I've been far more intimate with Linc than I was with either of the men I had intercourse with. He's helped me discover a side of myself I didn't know existed.

"Let's go, Trin!" he calls from a few feet in front of me.

My unenthusiastic groan comes out with one of my massive exhales. Linc has incredible stamina—he's a pro athlete. I swear he's actually enjoying this.

"Let's pick it up," he encourages.

If I had the breath to spare, I'd laugh. I must look ridiculous, red-faced and bundled up, huffing and puffing my way through knee-deep snow in my snowshoes.

Lincoln was so excited when he found those damn snowshoes in the storage room. I was, too. Past Trinity had no idea those shoes were actually instruments of torture.

"Think about your favorite song and let it push you," he says.

It reminds me that the entire world is moving every day while we're out here in this place where time doesn't really exist. Artists are releasing new music. Newscasters are reading the latest headlines.

Chicagoans are trudging through slushy gray melting snow to get to work and dinner and parties every day.

That was me before the plane crash. I lived my entire life on a schedule. I had my routine timed out perfectly, waking up at six fifteen on weekdays to get into the office. My workdays were scheduled out from the moment I walked in the door until I left in the evening. And then calendar reminders on my phone would tell me what time to meet colleagues or friends for drinks, when to pick up my dry cleaning and groceries—even phone calls with old friends were something I had to book time for in my schedule.

There's no schedule here. Every day is wide open.

Somehow I make it through five down and backs, and then Linc cleans the rabbit while I put on a Feist record and collapse onto the love seat.

Linc's right—I am getting better at exercise. If only I could reward myself with a chocolate shake.

While I work on making a stew with the rabbit, rice and canned beans and veggies, Linc fills the tub with water and I add bubbles. While the stew simmers on the hot plate, he gets in the tub and I sit between his legs, my back against his chest.

This is my favorite part of every day. Though we get more sunlight than we did when we first got here, we still spend more time in darkness than we do in the light. Every day, when the sun goes down, we put on a record and take a bath with just the light of a small lantern on the kitchen counter. It never stops being the most romantic thing I've ever done.

"What would you be doing right now at home?" I ask Linc.

I feel his hum against my back. "In March? Practicing. Working out. Maybe watching a show if I'm not on the road."

"Like *The Bachelor*?" I tease, craning my neck to make eye contact with him.

"Already told you, I'm not ashamed. The guys all know not to fuck with me when I'm watching it. That and *Survivor*."

"I like that you like *The Bachelor*, and you're secure enough in your manhood to admit it."

"Keep teasing me and you'll be choking on my manhood soon," he says lightly.

I laugh. "Oh, please. Don't threaten me with a good time."

He slides his hand over my upper thigh, his

other arm banding around my waist. I lean my head back against his chest, closing my eyes.

As his hand slowly moves closer to my inner thigh, I clench in anticipation. My body knows when Linc touches me, fireworks follow. Every single time.

I moan softly as he slides his fingers over and down, the pad of his middle finger gliding over my clit.

"Always ready, aren't you?" he murmurs in my ear.

"I could say the same for you." I wiggle my bottom slightly and he groans, his erection pressing against my back.

"It's impossible to see your hot body and not be hard as fuck."

His words send desire swirling low in my belly. Linc has changed the way I see myself. I never thought I was sexy until I started hearing him tell me pretty much every day that I am.

He reaches the hand around my waist up to lightly pinch my nipple. I arch my back, my exhale ragged.

"Such a hot little thing," he murmurs in my ear, his breath hot. "I love watching you come."

I pull my knees up to allow him greater access

as he circles my clit. I'm building toward an orgasm when he moves his hand down, putting two long fingers inside me.

I watch as his hand moves, moaning loudly when he grazes my clit. I move my hips shamelessly, desperate to increase the contact.

"Fuck my fingers, gorgeous." He squeezes my nipple harder this time, and I skate on the edge of release. "Get this sweet pussy off."

I shatter into a thousand pieces, crying out his name with my release. He keeps working his fingers until I relax against him. Then he kisses my temple and wraps his arms around me.

We lie in silence for a few minutes and I stroke my thumb over his knee. The record ends and I feel his stomach rumbling through my back.

I sit up and turn around. "Ready to wash?"

"I prefer you dirty." He winks and I feel a flutter in my stomach.

This is our ritual—he shampoos my hair and then I shampoo his. Then he washes my body and I wash his. We rarely make it out of the tub without both of us coming at least once.

Tonight is no exception. Once we're both clean, Linc stands up in the tub. Before he can step out, I get to my knees and put my hands on his ass, looking up at him.

"Fuck, babe." He runs a hand over my hair. "Are you serious?"

Instead of answering, I take him deep into my mouth to show him how serious I am. He groans loudly, moving his hand to the back of my head to grab a handful of my hair.

Even though he wore me out earlier with the workout, I always have enough energy for this. Hearing him react to what I'm doing makes me feel like an absolute *goddess*.

He tries to hold himself back, but soon he's pumping his hips, fisting my hair as he moves in and out of my mouth.

"You want it?" His voice is strained.

I can't answer, so I just moan my enthusiasm and in a few more seconds, he groans and comes in my mouth. I swallow it greedily.

Though I do fantasize about sex with him, what we have is incredible and it's enough for me. If we have to be stranded alone in a remote cabin, this is a hell of a way to pass the time.

twenty

LINCOLN

"Really?"

A couple days later, Trinity's face falls when she sees what I put on her plate for dinner.

"Look, I get it, but we both need to bulk up as much as we can before we leave. We need protein."

Dinner tonight is canned tuna, salmon jerky, black beans and mixed nuts. We've used most of the food in the cabin. Between that and the break in the weather, it's time for us to hike out of here.

We've started packing supplies, trying to include all the essentials and enough food to get us by. I figure we can cover about twenty miles a day, but we'll be hiking north, which should be the direction of Fairbanks, and it'll get colder as we go.

"I found my bracelet," Trin says as she sits down across from me at the table.

"Where was it?"

"In the kitchen drawer where the utensils are. It must've fallen off when I was getting something out of the drawer."

We turned the cabin upside down looking for that damn bracelet, a delicate silver chain. Trin was frantic when she realized it was missing a couple of days ago.

"Glad you found it."

I shovel a giant bite of canned tuna into my mouth, planning to finish it quickly. When we get back home, I'm eating at a steak house every night for a week. I spend a good part of every day fantasizing about a perfectly cooked medium rare filet, juice dripping off my fork as I raise it to my mouth.

"It's not valuable, but my dad gave it to me," Trin says as she picks up an almond from her plate.

"You don't talk about him much."

She shrugs. "I've been thinking about him more since we've been here. He took me and Dalton on fishing and hunting trips. He dreamed of going to Alaska one day to fish for salmon."

"You don't have to tell me if you don't want to, but was he sick, or did you lose him unexpectedly?"

"Kind of both. He was diagnosed with pancreatic cancer and he was gone less than a month later."

"Damn, I'm sorry."

She meets my gaze across the table. "You would've liked him. He never got frustrated with us, and if you knew how many times I got my fishing line tangled and he had to cut it and fix it, you'd be impressed by that."

"What was his name?"

"Mario." She picks up a hazelnut and puts it in her mouth. "Does Dalton talk about him?"

I shake my head. "I don't think I've ever heard him mention him. He talks about your mom, though."

Her eyes tear up at my mention of her mom.

"Our dad was Dalton's hero. He took his death really hard." She forces a smile. "What about your dad? Unless you don't want to say anything."

I sit up straighter and roll my shoulders, thoughts of my dad making me tense up. I've told

Trinity so much about myself, but my father is a subject that's hard for me to even think about.

"He, uh...left when I was ten." I scrub a hand down my face. "I mean, I thought he left."

She eats the food on her plate, letting me take time before I continue.

"My mom moved us from San Diego to Columbus and it was...sudden. She said Dad had a girlfriend and wanted to have a new family with her and her kids. And that we couldn't afford to live in San Diego anymore. We moved into a shitty little apartment and she got a job bartending. She told me and my sister that our dad never gave her a dime. Never tried to see us. I wouldn't have been able to keep playing hockey if not for scholarship programs."

I sigh heavily and look away.

Trinity covers my hand with hers. "You don't have to say anymore."

"No, I don't mind. My mom wasn't all bad. I don't mean to make it sound that way. She was a good mom and we loved her. But at her funeral, her sister told me she thought I deserved to know the truth, which was that my dad did ask for a divorce, but he never said he didn't want anything to do with me and my sister. He did pay child support and he tried to see us, but my mom wouldn't have it. She was so hurt that she hurt him back in the only way she could."

Trinity's lips turn down at the corners in a frown. "That's...I don't even know what to say."

"Yeah. I told myself at first that he must not have tried very hard, but when we were cleaning out Mom's house, I found all the birthday and Christmas cards and letters Dad had sent us. Just having those as a kid--" I stop talking, fighting a lump of emotion in my throat. "It would have meant a lot. To know my dad loved me. I wondered for all those years how he could just stop loving me."

"Have you ever tried to get in touch with him?"

I shake my head, shame washing over me. "I looked him up. He lives in Phoenix. Has a wife and another daughter. I thought about reaching out, but...I never did. And then our plane crashed and I thought I'd die without ever making things right with him."

She gets up and comes over to me, bending to hug me. The ends of her soft hair brush over my neck. "I'm so sorry. That's a heavy burden."

I rest my cheek against her chest. "When we

make it back, I'm going to call him. I don't even know what I'll say, but..."

She cups my face in her hands. "You'll know. When the time comes, the words will--"

A sound makes us both turn. When I see the front door moving, I realize the sound is someone opening it. I jump up from my chair to stand in front of Trin as a tall, twentysomething man walks inside and sees us.

"Are you fucking serious? Squatters?" He grabs a can of bear spray from a pocket in his cargo pants and points it at me. "I'll use this if I have to! You're trespassing."

I put a palm out to assure him I mean no harm. "Slow down, man. Don't fucking bear spray me. We were in a plane crash and we took shelter here. There weren't any other places to go. I've got the money to pay for everything we've used."

He pulls off a brown stocking cap and stuffs it into his pants, running his hand through unruly brown curly hair and glancing out the open doorway. "Cheri, there are squatters in here. Call the boss."

"A phone?" I take a few steps forward. "You guys have a phone? I'll pay you ten thousand bucks to make a phone call."

He moves the can of bear spray up and down. "Stay back! Let me guess, your plane was loaded up with drugs. If you've been making meth here, I swear to fuck I'll put my snow boot all the way up your ass. I'm not relocating to this tundra for a month to oversee the chemical cleanout. I almost turned feral when I had to oversee the solar panel install."

This guy looks—and sounds—more like Seth Rogen than Seth Rogen does. But I have more important things to discuss with him.

"Look, I'm Lincoln Rowe. I'm a pro hockey player for the Minnesota Mammoths. Google it and you'll find pictures of me without this caveman beard. We were in a plane crash in January. I have the money to pay for everything we used."

He lowers the bear spray slightly. "I don't think the sat phones can do that. I did hear about a hockey player in a plane crash, but I thought he died."

Trinity steps out from behind me, her hands out in front of her. "We would have died if we hadn't found this place. It saved our lives."

I bare my teeth to the guy, moving my lips so he can get a good look at them. "Look, dude. No meth. I've broken a few teeth playing hockey and gotten them fixed, but that's it."

He considers for a couple of seconds and then puts the can of bear spray back in a leg pocket of his pants. "Fucking nuts." He glances up at us. "Our boss will be here soon; he can give you a ride back to his plane."

Trinity laughs a single note. "I'm not getting on a plane. If we could just use a phone, that's all we need."

"Your boss has a plane?" I ask.

"What? Oh. Yeah. Cheri and I are two of his assistants. We always bring supplies in by snowmobile when he wants to spend time here."

Trin and I exchange a sheepish look.

"We've eaten most of the food," I say, stepping forward and extending my hand to him. "What was your name?"

"Logan." He pinches his brows together as he shakes my hand. "Sorry, the wheels are turning and I'm just thinking of stuff here...we're probably gonna need to call in legal and have you sign some paperwork."

"Uh...for what?"

He blows out a breath just as a petite woman walks into the cabin and smiles at us.

"Hi, I'm Cheri Marone, first assistant to Skyler Cross. Did I hear you say you're that hockey player from the plane crash in Alaska?"

Logan gives her an aggravated, wide-eyed look. "We said we were doing away with the whole first-assistant, second-assistant thing. We're both equal assistants."

"Skyler Cross?" My jaw drops. "You mean...?"

Cheri nods. "Yes, the tech billionaire. This is his cabin."

Logan throws his arms up and turns around. "I was going to have them sign NDAs before we told them that. You never ask for my input."

Trinity steps forward to introduce herself to Cheri. As they shake hands, she says, "You have nothing to worry about from us, I promise. This cabin saved our lives and we're completely indebted to Mr. Cross."

I put a palm on Trinity's back, the reality that we're being rescued starting to sink in. "I'll cover the costs of everything."

Cheri waves her hand dismissively. "That's not a concern. It's just that Mr. Cross comes here when he wants to be completely alone. Away from his crazy busy schedule. And if people knew about it--"

"It's a security risk," Logan finishes, his

forehead wrinkled with tension. "He's gonna want a whole new cabin built, isn't he?" He pinches the bridge of his nose. "I'll get assigned to Alaska again for *months*."

"Hey, *asshole*," Cheri snaps. "These two need medical attention. They need to call their families. None of this is about you."

He puts up his palms in surrender. "Right. You're right."

Trinity turns to me, tears brimming in her eyes. "We're going home!"

I hug her, relieved by our luck. Now we don't have to face the uncertainties of hiking out of here with supplies.

"You're the hockey player?"

I release Trinity and look at the cabin's doorway, where a very tall, lean man whose face I know well is standing. Skyler Cross is one of the wealthiest, most recognizable men in the world.

"That's me," I say.

He grins and unzips his thick parka. "What a world. Seattle's my team, but I couldn't be happier you two found refuge here."

Trinity rushes over to hug him. "Your cabin saved our lives, Mr. Cross. I don't even know how to thank you."

He gives her a fatherly look. "I'm just glad you found it. I think you're quite far from where they were searching for the plane." Feeling around in his coat pockets, he pulls out a satellite phone with a thick antenna. "Call your family, and then we'll get you both to my plane."

Trinity takes the phone, her expression turning wary. "I appreciate it, but I won't be able to get on a plane."

He nods. "Of course. I understand. We'll figure something out that you're comfortable with."

Cheri shows Trin how to dial the sat phone and I approach Skyler, shaking his hand. "We're so grateful for everything."

"It's my pleasure."

Trin walks to the other side of the cabin, the phone to her ear, as Cheri turns to me and Skyler.

"Um...Lincoln, we'd really appreciate you not mentioning the bear spray."

Skyler scrunches his forehead in confusion. "What bear spray?"

Cheri looks up at her boss, who's a solid foot taller than her. "Logan pulled bear spray on them when we walked in."

Skyler rolls his eyes. "Please tell me he didn't spray any of it."

I answer. "No, and it's forgotten, really. I know it was alarming to walk in and see two strangers eating at the kitchen table."

The subject is forgotten when I hear Trinity crying. I turn to look at her and she's facing me, tears streaming down her face. "We're okay, Dalton. We're both just fine. I'm so sorry for the way I treated you the last time I saw you. You were—" She pauses to listen. "I know. I love you, too."

I smile at her, the fact that it's over sinking all the way in. Using an outhouse, never being completely warm and eating tuna out of a can as a main course—all over.

I'll go back to my life in Minneapolis, to my team. And Trin will go back to her life in Chicago. I knew it had to happen at some point, but I didn't expect to feel such a stab of regret over it.

It's us—me and her—that's the only thing I regret being over.

twenty-one

TRINITY

I OPEN MY EYES AND THEY IMMEDIATELY FALL closed again. My eyelids feel like lead.

"Linc?" I try to say his name, but I can't seem to get my mouth to work like I want it to.

Though I can't see him, I hear his voice. He's right next to me. "Everything's good, Trin. Go back to sleep." A brief pause, and then, "She might need some more of that medicine; she's waking up."

I'm in a hospital bed. I can tell from the feel of the bed and the smell of the air around me—like plastic tubing and lemon cleaner.

"Mom, she's awake."

When I turn toward the voice, Dalton is sitting there, one of my hands cradled in both of his.

"Dalton."

My eyes fill with tears. His hair is a little shorter and he has the shadow of a couple days' beard growth, but otherwise he looks the same.

"Oh, my girl." Our mom walks up to the other side of the bed, tears on her cheeks.

There's a lot more gray in her hair than I remember. Her face, which was lean before, is now almost sunken, dark circles beneath her eyes.

I reach out to her. "Mom, are you okay?"

She smiles at me, fresh tears flooding her eyes. "Of course I am. Now that I know you're okay, I'm just fine."

She picks up a cup of water with a straw in it from the table next to my bed, holding it in front of my mouth so I can take a drink.

"Where am I?"

Dalton answers. "A hospital in Seattle."

I have no idea what day it is. Skyler Cross's team called for rescuers, and Lincoln and I were taken from the cabin to Fairbanks by a team of paramedics on snowmobiles. We were evaluated at a hospital in Fairbanks, where we got the bad news that we couldn't drive to our homes because we didn't have passports to get through Canada. There was no choice but to fly on a plane.

That was when I started to melt down inside from my anxiety, and it's also when Lincoln gently asked me if I wanted medication to make things easier.

I asked to be sedated for the flight if possible, and it seems that the rescue team understood the assignment. I have no memory of even seeing a plane. Was I even on one?

"Did I come here on a plane?" I croak.

My brother smiles at me. "Yep. Linc said you only woke up a little bit one time. And you're doing fine, just getting some nutrients in the IV. When you get released, Mom will drive you back to Chicago in a rental car."

I just stare at him, still feeling woozy. "Where's Linc?"

"He's here in another room. They're working on his release paperwork. Unfortunately, I can't be here much longer because he and I have to get back to the team."

My eyes widen with alarm. Lincoln is *leaving?* And his team expects him to go play hockey?

"How long have I been out?"

Dalton checks his watch. "You got here a couple of hours ago. So not that long."

"So...you and Linc are going to play a game."

He grins. "Well, I will. It's a little more complicated for Linc because he's not on our roster right now. But our coaches and owner want him back so our doctors can take a look at him."

I let my head fall back against the pillow. Everything happened so quickly, and then I was asleep for the rest of it. I still can't believe we've been rescued and we don't have to hike into the unknown.

"Is Karma okay?"

Mom pats my arm reassuringly. "She's fine. I took her to live with me after the plane crash. She shredded every curtain in my house."

I crack a smile. "Sorry. You know what they say about Karma."

She shrugs. "We have an understanding."

Dalton grins at her. "Meaning she doesn't have any curtains anymore, just blinds."

A nurse carries a huge box into the room and

sets it on a chair. "Glad to see you up, Trinity. I'm going to check your vitals."

"What's in the box?"

"No idea. It was delivered for you a few minutes ago by one of our security guards."

After she takes my vital signs, a doctor comes in to check me. She tells me I seem perfectly healthy but slightly anemic.

"Have a nice big steak when you leave here," she suggests with a smile.

My lips part. "Food! I can have bread. And ice cream. I'm never eating another bite of canned tuna."

"What can I order for you before I have to head out?" my brother asks. "Anything in all of Seattle, just say the word and it's yours."

My mouth waters as I think about the options. Linc and I sometimes played a game at the cabin we called "food fantasy," where we would each think up a complete menu for a meal and vote on whose was best. Not surprisingly, it was often a tie.

"A sub sandwich on freshly baked bread. With roast beef, ham, provolone, that oil dressing stuff and pickles."

"That's oddly specific," Dalton says.

"And a chocolate milkshake with lots of whipped cream. No cherry."

He gives me a fond look and then comes over to hug me. "I'm on it. I'm so glad you're back. We never gave up hope, but...it was getting tough."

"I prayed every day," my mom says. "My knees ached from praying so hard. I knew God would watch over you, though."

The nurse comes back into the room, wearing a look of disappointment. "Hey, I just want to let you know we've got a lot of reporters looking for you and the other survivor. We aren't letting them past the lobby and we don't give away any patient information to nonfamily members. Our PR team will coordinate your releases through a private parking garage beneath the hospital. We use it to sneak high-profile patients in and out."

I sit up in bed, running my hands over my hair. "I want to see Linc before he leaves."

Dalton walks over to the doorway of my room. "I'll tell him. I'm going to see him now and I'll order your food."

"Hey, before you go, will you open that box?"

"Yep." Dalton goes over to the box and tears into it the same way I remember him opening boxes when we were kids.

He pulls out a small jar of face cream and a card. "Seems to be full of toiletries. Someone's trying to tell you you stink, Trin."

"La Mer!" The sight of my favorite moisturizer sends a wave of longing through me. "Please, can I smell it?"

Wrinkling his brow, he brings me the cream and the card. "Have at it, weirdo. I'm going to get your food."

I open the envelope and take out the card inside it.

Dearest Trinity,

I cried grateful tears when I heard the news you've been found and you're okay. We miss you greatly here at the office. You have a job here always, but take the time you need before you come back. I'm sending a few essentials. Call when you can.

Gloria

"From my boss," I tell my mom. "Will you show me what else is in there?"

It's been so long since I've been around beauty products that I'd forgotten how much I love them. I ooh and ahh over the assorted shampoos, conditioners, body washes, lipsticks and other items. There's even a plush pale-purple robe and slippers.

"Do you think they'd let me take a shower?"

Mom asks the nurse, who helps me get into the bathroom with my IV pole for a one-armed shower. It's glorious. I lather my body and hair several times, deep condition my hair and exfoliate my face. Gloria even made sure I had a fresh toothbrush and toothpaste. So when I walk out of the bathroom, I'm clean and moisturized from head to toe. I feel like a new person.

"That was heaven," I say, assuming my mom is still in the room.

Instead, it's Linc who stands up from sitting in the chair in the corner, his lips quirking up in a smile as he looks me over in my purple robe and slippers. "You look cute."

I stop brushing my wet hair and just look at him for a few seconds. We haven't been apart for very long, but it feels like we have.

He showered, too, and his face is clean-shaven. He's wearing a pair of surgical scrubs.

"I wanted to see you before I leave," he says, his expression turning serious.

My heart sinks. I knew this had to happen, but it feels more alarming than I thought it would.

"I have so much to say that I don't even know where to begin," I say. "And also, I have nothing to say. Is that weird?"

The corners of his eyes crinkle when he smiles. I'm going to miss those crinkles. "Not at all. I feel the same way. I got your number from Dalton, though, so obviously, I'll call you."

I nod, looking at the ground and then back up at him. "Does he...know?"

He shrugs. "He pretty much guessed when the doctors had to forcibly remove me from your room when we got here, but we didn't talk about it a lot."

"You're doing okay, though?"

"Yeah. Everything's a little overwhelming, but...I'm good. How about you? Any aftereffects from the sedation?"

"I am pretty tired. But I'm going to wait for my sub sandwich before I go back to sleep. If you hear a woman orgasming loudly on your way out here, that's me when I take my first bite of bread in three months."

His eyes twinkle. "I definitely know what that sounds like."

There's a flip in my stomach. I have so many questions, but I can't ask any of them. Someone knocks on the door and Lincoln calls out. "Give us a minute. Almost done."

He comes over to me. "I have to go. The team sent PR people and it sounds like getting out of here is going to be a thing. We're going to have a blond intern from the hospital leave with us, so hopefully the reporters will think it's you and leave."

I won't let myself cry. This should be a moment of celebration, not a time for tears. This is everything we wanted—we were rescued. But deep down inside myself, in a place I don't want anyone to see, it feels like a part of me is about to walk out the door.

He steps forward to hug me, and I fly into his arms. He holds me tightly, sighing heavily.

"I'll miss you, Trin."

"I'll miss you, too." So much for not crying; my tears are leaking onto the shoulder of his scrub shirt.

"I'll call you soon. And if you need anything, anytime, call me." He takes a half step back, cradling my face in his hands. "Tell me you'll call me, even if it's two in the morning and you just want to ask what flavor of Oreos you should eat."

I smile through my tears. "The ones with the chocolate stuffing are the best. I dream of a world where I can get double-stuffed chocolate stuffing. And yes, I'll call. Same goes for you, okay?"

He leans his forehead against mine. "Yeah. And about the guy who was stalking you...I hired a private detective agency to follow him around the clock for a while. I don't want either of us worrying about that on top of everything else. If he tries to get close to you, they'll intervene."

Either of us. How did I not immediately fall for him?

"I don't know what to say, Linc, other than thank you."

The knock on the door is louder this time. He glares at the back of the door.

"You better go," I say.

He kisses my forehead. "I'll call you. Get some sleep. After your sandwich."

I nod and he steps away. He takes my hand and squeezes it, holding on until he has to let go as he walks toward the door.

"Bye, Trin."

I hold up a hand. "Bye, Linc."

He walks out the door, closing it behind him. I sit down on the edge of my bed, reality setting in.

Lincoln's gone. Our cabin fling is just a memory now.

twenty-two

LINCOLN

MY TEAMMATES GAPE AT ME WHEN I WALK INTO THE locker room, our goalie Lucas wiping the corner of his eye.

"You are the ugliest fuckin' ghost I've ever seen," Archer Holt says, approaching me with open arms and a grin.

When I hug him, the room seems to collectively exhale. I step back and look around at all the faces I wasn't sure I'd ever see again when Trin and I were searching for shelter.

I told her a lot about my teammates when we were at the cabin. Not just their individual personalities but also stories from the locker room, games and vacations we've taken together.

Dane Foster, whose devil-may-care attitude means he's usually the talk of the team, embraces me tightly. He was hospitalized with alcohol poisoning on a summer trip to Mexico, and none of us were surprised he hooked up with one of his nurses during this stay—and got her to sneak him a beer.

"Great to have you back, cap." He embraces me and claps me on the back. "It wasn't the same without you."

"I mean, you don't look bad for a dead guy." Aaron Parker puts his hands on my shoulders and grins at me. "You're an absolute legend, man."

Every one of my teammates joined the search for the plane after the crash. Dalton told me all about it on our flight from Seattle to Tampa to meet up with our team. They flew back to Alaska on the team plane and searched until they had to fly out for their next game, and then they returned to search some more after that.

"You didn't get frostbite, did you?" Aiden Rogers gives me a serious look. "We won't judge if part of your dick fell off."

"Eat shit. I could lose half of mine and it'd still

be bigger than yours." We both bust out laughing and embrace each other.

Dalton hangs back, probably because he's already had lots of time to catch up with me. I'm concerned about him. He's leaner and his eyes have a haunted look. I think he's been holding himself responsible for what happened to me and Trin, even though none of it was his fault.

Once I've greeted everyone, I sit down in a chair by the training room, needing a minute to myself. I won't be dressing for games until I've been medically cleared, which will be a process. The doctors in Seattle released me, but it'll take a lot more to get cleared to play hockey again.

Will I be the same? I haven't gone more than ten days without a stick in my hand since I was eight years old—until now. And going ten days was rare. I'll still know how to play, obviously, but will I be as fast? As sharp?

I'm only five goals away from the Mammoths' team record for most goals scored by a single player. And since I could be traded, this season is my chance to clinch it. I should be able to get medically cleared soon since I worked to keep myself in shape at the cabin. And then I know my teammates will have my back as I chase the record.

"Lincoln, welcome back! We have so much to discuss!"

I look up to see Tamara Curtis, the Mammoths' head of PR, standing right in front of me, a clipboard tucked against her chest.

Her voice sounds like a chirping bird. This isn't what I had in mind for my few moments of quiet.

"Hey, Tamara. Thanks. I'm not officially back yet."

She sits down next to me. "Which works out perfectly because it gives us time to get in some interviews before you start dressing again. I'm thinking of giving Nikki Curtis the first interview. She wants you to bring anything you have from the day of the crash, like torn clothes, that you can show her on camera. She's working on getting Trinity Lorenzo, too. I don't know if she'll want you to sit down for the interview together, but probably?"

I bristle. Trinity is still in the hospital. She's not something for some vulture reporter to "get" so they can maximize clicks and views.

"No, we're not doing that."

Tamara pinches her brows together. "If you need to catch up on sleep first, I tot--"

"No. No interviews."

She opens her mouth to say something, closes it, and then opens it again. "Is there anything I need to know about your...experience? Something that could make the team look bad if it's discovered?"

My lips part with surprise. "My *experience*? We almost died. How could that make the team look bad?"

"I don't know." She puts her hands up in mock surrender. "I'm just saying, the press is foaming at the mouth for details about where you've been and what happened. This interview is a way for you to get the story out there."

"The *story*?" Anger tightens my chest. "This isn't a story; it's my life. Trinity's life. And no one gets to know anything about any of it unless we choose to tell them."

A few of my teammates are glaring at Tamara. Dalton approaches the two of us, standing next to my chair.

"This isn't a good time, Tamara."

She presses her lips together. "I guess just...let me know when it is a good time."

"Never," I say darkly, standing up. "Don't come at me about this ever again."

"I'm just doing my job."

I don't even bother responding. Instead, I go

into the weight room, which is mercifully empty. I sit down on a bench, elbows on my spread knees.

Someone sits down nearby after following me into the room. I look up to see Dalton.

"This is all a lot, yeah?"

I sigh heavily and sit up. "Yeah. The cabin was quiet and peaceful, Just the two of us. And we didn't expect to get whisked out of there like that." I snap my fingers.

"You know you don't have to be here, right? You can get on a plane right now and fly home. Coach will understand."

I shake my head. "What would I do there? Go grocery shopping? Watch TV? Nothing feels right."

Dalton meets my gaze. "Why don't you call Trin and talk to her about it?"

"Maybe I will. I do want to check on her."

"Look, you're my best friend. Let's just get it out there—you and my sister aren't just friends."

My lack of an answer *is* my answer.

"I knew it from the time I walked into her hospital room and she kept asking where you were and wanting to see you."

"It didn't happen right away. I tried to stay away because she's your sister, but..." I shake my head. "I don't know, I guess I was weak."

"I'm not pissed."

My brows hit my hairline. "You're not?"

He shakes his head. "Before any of this happened, I would've ripped your balls off for sleeping with my sister. But I spent the better part of three months thinking you were both dead. The searchers told us after a week that there was very little chance you guys survived and I didn't want to give up hope, but..." He looks away. "I can't even describe the way it feels to imagine your sister and best friend knowing they're about to die in a plane crash. Wondering if it was quick or if you guys suffered. Going to memorial services for both of you. My mom..." He clears his throat. "You guys went through something horrific, and I'm..." He wipes the corners of his eyes, his voice thick with emotion. "I'm really fucking glad you had each other."

"You know none of this was your fault, right?"

He gives me a weak smile. "Yeah, I'm in therapy over it. But I appreciate you saying it."

"So here's the crazy thing...a few parts of it were horrific. The crash, obviously. And I got lost when I went looking for help and was pretty sure I was done for. But most of it...wasn't bad at all. It was actually...good."

"Really?" Dalton's brow furrows with surprise. "Yeah, once we found the cabin. We listened to records and danced, talked, played Boggle, cooked...we got sick of rice and beans, but we were glad to have food. We took baths. Laughed."

"Baths?"

I nod. "Hot baths. Perk of finding a billionaire's cabin."

"Oh shit. Was this like a luxury hunting lodge?"

"No, not at all. It was simple. Small. We had to use an outhouse and there was only one lamp. But it was everything we needed."

"Are you in love with her?"

I lock my eyes on his. "Yeah, I think I am."

"How's that gonna work? She's in Chicago and you're in Minneapolis. Or on the road."

I shrug. "I never said anything about it working. But no one knows me the way she does. No one else could get how I'm feeling right now. It's like part of me is missing."

A few seconds of silence pass.

"Does she feel the same way?"

"I have no idea. We never talked about it."

"You should talk to her."

I stand up and pace to the other side of the empty weight room. "I don't even know what I'd be asking her for. It doesn't feel fair to ask her to move when she has a life and a career in Chicago."

"You can't move there, though."

"Yeah." I look away. "I want to talk to her, but it feels more like an in-person conversation."

"Are you sure things will be the same between the two of you when you're living a regular life instead of a permanent honeymoon in a cabin? When you're stinking up the bathroom and gone for road trips more than half of the time?"

I scoff. "You know me. I'm not a relationship guy. I don't have the answers to any of this. I'm just telling you--"

There's a knock on the locker room door, and Dane opens it and looks between us. "Time to go, ladies."

We both stand up. Even though I'm not dressed in my uniform, I'm sitting with the team in an assistant coaching capacity tonight. One of the other assistants gave up his spot for me. I even had to borrow his dress clothes, and the shirt's too tight in the arms and too big in the waist.

But I get to be with my team. They were insistent that I be with them tonight. Tomorrow, I'll start practicing again and undergoing the tests I need to be cleared to play.

Dalton claps a hand on my shoulder as we walk out of the room.

I want to call Trin, but I don't know what to say. I need to figure things out myself before I can talk to her about any of it.

I force it from my mind as we leave the locker room to head for the ice. I've made this walk many times, but it feels different this time. Like I'm not a member of the team but just there to support them.

The lights of the arena flash and blink brightly, the crowd roaring and the music pumping. It's the polar opposite of the cabin, where soft music flowed from the record player as I danced with the woman whose body fit perfectly against mine, her cheek on my shoulder and her breath on my neck.

Impossible as it seems, or the next three hours, I have to focus on hockey.

twenty-three

TRINITY

"Are you sure you want to be here?"

My coworker and friend, Genevieve, gives me a concerned look as she sips her coffee from the chair on the other side of my desk. Which is also kind of *her* desk because she was moved into my job a couple of months ago, but Gloria is letting us share the job for now.

"I have three months' worth of catching up to do. And I can't get a moment of peace at my apartment, anyway."

There are a handful of reporters and photographers who have made it their mission to take photos of me and shout questions at me every time I go in and out of my apartment. I'm grateful for Gideon and Brielle, the bodyguards who switch off escorting me everywhere. Linc hired them because of Ronan, but I need them to fend off not just the reporters but also people I pass on the street who recognize me and take photos.

The story of our rescue is *everywhere*. I have a new phone, but I keep it set to silent and only use it for phone calls and texts because social media is overwhelming in every possible way right now.

"You need to come stay with me," Genevieve says for at least the fifth time.

"Then they'll just wait for me outside of your door."

"They'll have to go through me first."

"I missed you." I set down the latte she brought me a few minutes ago. "And I'm sorry, but I can't drink this. I'm not used to this much sugar anymore."

She waves a hand. "No worries, I'll ask you what you want next time."

It's my second day back at the office. After two days in the hospital in Seattle, my mom drove me home and stayed with me for three days. She cooked my favorite foods—pasta carbonara, steak and even a chocolate cheesecake—and we binge-watched shows from my couch.

I haven't gotten to see Karma yet because he's back at my mom's staying with one of her friends. But the time alone with my mom was better than any time I've ever spent with her. She didn't fuss over my apartment and I wasn't petty toward her. It seems like we both know now that life's too short for any of that.

"I can't believe these numbers," I tell Genevieve as I look over the sales figures for Allura's first two full months of sales. "They're above and beyond anything I anticipated."

"You had all the pieces in place."

I laugh off her compliment. "No, this was a team effort. I had myself convinced the launch couldn't be successful if...well, *if a hundred different things*. But you guys did an amazing job."

"I'm not keeping the job," she blurts. "This is your job and I don't want you to think I just swooped in and took it. I cried every day of my first week in this office."

I smile and meet her gaze. "I'd never think that. The show must go on."

"Well, it's your job and your office. There are

openings on Patrick's team; he already said I can have a spot if I want it."

"Let's not talk about that yet."

"Okay, but can we talk about you being trapped in a cabin with a hot hockey player? Was there only one bed?"

My cheeks warm and she squeals with excitement. "I knew it! Tell me everything."

The two of us have always shared all the details of our lives with each other, but for some reason, I feel protective of every moment I've spent with Lincoln. It wasn't salacious or even about sex. We needed each other.

And now it's over. I think about him constantly, especially when I'm lying in bed alone at night. I'd trade the bed in my heated bedroom to be back in the cabin's bed with him in a heartbeat. I miss the feel of his strong arms around me, the wind whipping against the cabin's walls. The sound of him groaning when he's about to come. The feel of his chiseled chest behind my back in the bathtub, his hands roaming over my bare skin.

How could I possibly put all of that into words Genevieve would understand? I don't even understand it myself—I just *feel* it, deep inside.

"Later," I tell her. "I seriously have so much work to catch up on."

"Gloria doesn't expect you to catch up on three months' worth of work in a matter of days, you know. Be gentle with yourself."

I glance at my phone screen, hoping to see a text from Linc. Nothing.

We've texted a few times and had one awkward phone conversation because my mom could hear me talking to him and I was guarded. He's been traveling with his team since.

"Are you okay?" Genevieve asks me, her tone laced with concern.

"Hmm?" I tuck my phone back into my bag. "Yeah, I'm good."

"Are you, though? You just don't seem like yourself."

I shrug and sigh. "It's harder than I thought it would be to get back into my old routine. I don't know if my meds are built up enough in my system to be effective yet."

When the doctor in Seattle put me back on my anxiety medication, I nearly cried with relief. I was managing my anxiety as well as I could with meditation and deep breathing, but it was still there. I know the medication is at least helping me because I don't feel as on edge as I did when I first got home.

I'm still not the same, though. I keep waiting to wake up one morning and feel exactly like I did before Alaska—excited about the workday ahead, thinking about my plans for the weekend.

It's Friday, and I'll be spending this weekend alone in my apartment. All the friends who have reached out to me since I got back just want to talk about the plane crash and the cabin. I understand their curiosity, but they ask questions I don't feel ready to answer.

"How can I help?" Genevieve asks.

I smile softly. "I don't know. Just listen when I need it, I guess. I appreciate you asking."

"Let's hang out this weekend. We'll do whatever you feel like."

I think about it for a few seconds. "Yoga might be nice. And maybe breakfast after at that place with the huge pastries."

"That sounds like a plan."

"My mom is flying back on Sunday to bring Karma home."

"Oh, Karma." She puts her palm to her chest. "How much have you missed her?"

"I can't wait to see her. She's my snuggle buddy."

An intern knocks on the office door and then opens it, her gaze going straight to me when she walks in. She wasn't working here before the plane crash, and she stares at me like I'm a sideshow oddity.

"Miss Lorenzo, you have several phone messages." She passes me the slips of paper.

"Do we not do phone messages over email anymore?"

"Oh, sorry. I thought you didn't have an email address anymore."

I nod. "You're right, my fault. Thanks for these."

The IT department shut down my email address after my memorial service. Linc and I weren't declared legally dead, which would have created a ton of red tape to undo. Dalton said the rescue team wanted to wait until the snow thawed and then resume searching for our bodies.

"It's pretty morbid being presumed dead," I murmur when the intern is gone.

"I can't even imagine." Genevieve gives me a sympathetic look.

I rub my temple, fighting the urge to check my

phone again for a text from Linc. As difficult as it is, I have to find a way to get back in my old groove.

"Can you go over the financial presentation from last month's board meeting for me?"

Genevieve grins widely. "Financials, my favorite! I thought you were going to want to do something boring, like cut out of here for chips, queso and margaritas." She shivers. "I'd much rather talk profit-and-loss statements."

I shake my head, smiling. "What if we multitask and you tell me about it over the queso and margaritas?"

She lights up. "Done!"

We make our way out of the office, my coworkers not so covertly staring at me as we walk by their cubicles.

"Can I help you with something?" Genevieve snaps at a woman whose mouth is hanging open as she watches me.

The woman quickly turns away and resumes her paperwork.

"Idiots," my friend mutters.

She puts her arm through mine and gives me a reassuring smile. What would I do without her? I already miss Linc so much; it's all I can do not to break down and cry in my office. It's going to take time for me to find normalcy again, and it won't be the routine I've come to crave with Linc.

Maybe it'll never be like it was before. Maybe I'm different now, and I'll have to find a brand-new normal for myself. I hadn't gone a day without serums, cleansers, moisturizers and cosmetics in years when I ended up stranded without access to any of them. I felt naked at first, like my bare skin wasn't really *me* anymore.

And while I've loved every second of my hot showers with foaming soap and the thick, rich moisturizer I apply since getting home, I had to force myself to put on makeup before I came to the office today.

The things that are important to me have changed. Unfortunately, something that's become deeply important to me is a tall, dark-haired hockey player who lives in another state.

I reach into my bag and wrap my hand around my phone, itching to call him and ask if he misses me, too.

But I don't. He has my number. If he wanted to call, he would.

At least I have Genevieve. And soon Karma. And of course, queso and margaritas. I'll be leaning on all of them as I find my new normal.

twenty-four

NINE DAYS LATER

LINCOLN

Nervousness ripples through my chest as I step out of my Uber and murmur my thanks to the driver. Trinity's tall, dark brick apartment building in Wrigleyville is on a tree-lined street with a few people walking dogs and riding bikes.

I've imagined where she lives so many times. I pictured a sterile high-rise, but this is definitely more her.

Taking a deep breath, I walk up the front stairs and enter the key code Dalton gave me to get in the front door. I think she's home because I called her when my flight landed. She thought I was calling from a road trip to Vancouver with the team.

When I climb the stairs to the second floor, a burly man dressed all in black stands up from the chair he's sitting in beside her apartment door.

"Can I help you, man?" he asks.

"You must be Gideon." I offer him my hand and he shakes it, giving me a wary look. "I'm Lincoln, the one who hired you through the agency."

"I'll need to see some ID. It's standard procedure."

Guess he wouldn't be much of a bodyguard if he just took my word for it. "Uh, yeah. I'll get my license." I pass him the bouquet of roses I'm holding.

Once I show him my license, he nods and passes back the flowers.

"I still need Miss Lorenzo to approve you," he says.

"Yeah, of course." I reach for the doorbell, then remember the sandwich I ate at the airport.

I flash Gideon a huge smile. "Do I have anything in my teeth?"

He lowers his brows in annoyance. "No."

I put my hand in front of my mouth and blow into it, trying to check my breath.

"Don't ask me to smell your breath," he mutters. "I've got mints if you want one."

"That'd be great."

He passes me a couple of Tic Tacs and I chew them up, not wanting to have them in my mouth when I kiss Trin. I'm nervous as a high school kid picking up his prom date.

When I ring the doorbell, she opens the door and gapes at me.

"Linc!" Her hands fly to her hair, which is piled on top of her head in a wild bun. She has green stuff all over her face and is wearing boxers and a worn navy T-shirt that says "Calm Your Tits." "No!"

Before I can get a word out, she slams the door in my face.

I turn to Gideon and he shrugs, trying to suppress a smile.

"Don't leave!" Trin yells from the other side of the door. "Just give me a minute!"

I stand there with Gideon for almost five minutes, making small talk about hockey and the weather. When the door finally opens again, Trinity is smiling.

"Hello," she says smoothly.

Her face has been scrubbed clean and her hair is loose around her shoulders. She's wearing black leggings and a plain gray V-neck T-shirt.

"Hey." I grin at her. "Who was that who opened your door before? I didn't recognize her."

She waves dismissively. "Oh, no one you'd know. What are you doing? Get in here!"

Gideon is forgotten as I walk inside, using my foot to push the door closed as I wrap my arms around her. She smells lightly of soap and something sweet and tropical. All my fears that this wouldn't be a pleasant surprise fade as she looks up at me, her eyes bright.

"I can't believe you're here."

"I can't believe it took me this long to figure my shit out and get here."

I release her and set the bouquet of roses down on a chair. A gray cat cocks its head at me from its perch on top of a nearby love seat.

"Karma." I grin and gently pet the cat's head.

Then I return to Trin and bend slightly before picking her up. She squeals and wraps her legs around my waist. I kiss her and she puts her arms around my neck.

She slides her hand around to my cheek as we

kiss, then pulls away and rests her forehead against mine.

"No beard," she murmurs against my lips.

"You like me better with or without it?"

"I like you both ways. How did you get out of going to Vancouver?"

"It was actually really easy. I just retired."

Her jaw drops as she pulls back to get a look at my full face. "What?"

My heart pounds hard. I have so much to tell her, but my body's in no mood for talking. She's wrapped around me, her perfect ass in my hands and her breasts just inches away.

"I'll tell you all about it," I promise. "But first, I want my retirement gift."

"Your gift?" She hikes up her brows in alarm. "But I didn't--"

I interrupt her. "Oh, you've got something for me, gorgeous. It's wrapped in black pants and a gray T-shirt."

The corners of her lips turn up in a sexy smile. "And you're going to unwrap it?"

I peek around her shoulder in search of a hallway. "Soon as I find your bedroom."

Her apartment is small, with oak hardwood floors and two big windows in the living room. The kitchen just has the basics and is open to the living room. Framed vintage cosmetics ads adorn the walls and there are pillows and blankets scattered all over the living room furniture.

"It's the doorway on the right. The other one's the bathroom."

I start walking that direction. She puts her hands on my cheeks and looks into my eyes.

"I thought you sounded weird on the phone. Is this why?"

"Yeah." I grin. "I was afraid you'd be able to tell from the background noise that I was at an airport."

Her expression turns serious. "I may need to think about this, actually. I'm still young. In my prime, really. Should I be fucking around with a *retiree*?"

I roar with laughter and smack her ass as I walk into her bedroom. The unmade queen-size bed takes up most of the tiny room. I set her on it and she grins up at me playfully.

I pull a box of condoms from my pocket and hold it up for her to see. "I had more than fucking around in mind, so think fast, gorgeous."

Her smile is replaced by a serious look, her eyes wide. "Linc...are you sure?"

I tear open the box, looking down at her as she leans up on her elbows. "I've done a lot of thinking in the past couple of weeks. And here are the things I'm sure of, I'm done with hockey and I want this with you, more than anything. I love you, Trin. I want a future with you."

Tears pool in her eyes. "I love you, too. I haven't been able to stop thinking about you."

Setting the condoms down, I move on top of her, supporting my weight on my elbows as I kiss her. Immediately, I know this is right.

My teammates back home were in a state of shock when I announced my retirement. I got cleared medically to return to playing, but after a couple weeks of sitting with my team in arenas with flashing lights and pounding music, I didn't want to go back.

I'm done chasing wins and records. I miss the quiet peace of my time with Trin at the cabin.

I kiss every inch of her as I remove her clothes, aching to bring her pleasure. She allowed me past the walls she'd built, and I want to do the same for her.

She stiffens nervously as I lower my face to the apex of her thighs. I sit up, my knees on the bed, and put one of her legs over my shoulder, kissing her calf.

"Don't be nervous," I murmur, running my hand from her ankle, up her calf, to her thigh.

She meets my gaze. "I feel like...in Alaska, I was a different person. Uninhibited. With nothing to lose. But in my own bedroom, I'm the person I've always been."

Moving my free hand between her legs, I slowly run the backs of my fingers up and down the seam of her pussy. She gasps and closes her eyes.

"You'll never lose me, Trin. I know you. I know your body and I want you more than any other woman on this planet."

I put a finger inside her and she moans. My cock is straining in my jeans, my fantasies about being inside her finally on the verge of coming true. When I circle her clit with my thumb, she bites her lip and moans again.

"Open your eyes, gorgeous." I put my thumb in my mouth and thoroughly wet it, then return it to her clit.

Her eyes fly open as I circle it, her lips parting as she meets my gaze. This is one of my favorite things about her. She starts off shy, but once I get her turned on, she forgets all her inhibitions and gives herself over to me.

"Not from this," she pants, scooting back slightly. "I want to come when you're inside me."

I move from the bed, enjoying the way she watches me as I pull off my shirt and unbutton my jeans. I want this with every cell of my body. I never thought I could feel the sense of rightness I have with her.

I put a condom on, hoping I don't suck at this since it's been so long. But when I slide inside her and we both groan, all my fears and insecurities disappear.

She puts her arms around my back, pulling me down closer, and I drive my hips into hers. Her little moans of pleasure are almost too much. I want to stretch it out for as long as possible and pound into her as hard as I can, both at the same time.

"Feels so good, Linc," she says in my ear. "Please don't stop. I want to be the only woman you come inside of."

"Oh, fuck."

It's all I can do to hold on as she grinds her hips up into mine, working herself against me in time to every thrust. The second she arches her back and moans loudly, I bury myself in her, not stopping even as I come. I don't want to cut her orgasm short.

"I've got some work to do on longevity," I say as I move off her. "Sorry about that."

She laughs lightly. "Stop it. We both came and seeing as it's been nine years for you, you did amazing."

I kiss her. "It'll be better next time. And even better the time after that."

"You've never once disappointed me in bed. You're the best I've ever had by miles, and you know it."

I lean up on an elbow, running my fingertips over her rounded breasts and perfectly pink nipples. "The best, huh? Maybe we should discuss that further."

She gives me a gentle shove on the shoulder. "I've told you that many times. And I'm not even hurt that you've never said it to me."

"Haven't I?" I think about it.

She waves a hand. "No, it's fine. I'm sure, as a hockey player, you've been with women who have sucked thousands of dicks. They're pro level."

I put my hand on her cheek and gently move her face until our eyes meet. "You're the only woman I've ever been in love with like this, Trin.

The only one I've ever been able to see myself with forever. I want you and only you."

Her gaze softens. "You haven't let on any of this when we've talked on the phone and texted. I'm shocked, to be honest with you. I mean, very pleasantly shocked, but...shocked."

"I needed time to figure things out. I didn't plan to retire for another two or three years, and I didn't want to ask you to move unless I knew I could give you everything."

She smiles. "And now you can move to Chicago. I didn't think any of this was even an option until you knocked on my door, so I know I might seem a little...dazed. But I feel it, too. I knew I was in love with you before we got rescued. A part of me didn't want to leave, crazy as it sounds."

"Not crazy at all."

"I can't wait to introduce you to my coworkers and friends. You're going to love my neighbor Rina. I know my apartment is really small, but the cabin was smaller and we were happy there. Do you want to move in?"

Tonight isn't the time to tell her I'm not moving to Chicago. Tonight is just about finally being together. I kiss her and slide my hand around to her back, then down to her ass.

"What I want is to take a bath with you. I miss playing with your pussy."

She hums her agreement against my lips. "No bathtub here. How about a shower?"

"That'll work."

twenty-five

TRINITY

Sunlight spills in around the edges of the curtains through the window in my bedroom the next morning. I just turned off my alarm and I curl back into Linc, wishing I could go back to sleep.

We had a ridiculous amount of crazy good sex, taking the occasional break to rejuvenate with snuggling or a late-night snack. I had to reluctantly tell him around three a.m. that I needed to get a little sleep. I have a huge work meeting today.

That three and a half hours was the best I've slept since I got back home. I fell asleep immediately and didn't have nightmares.

"Call in sick," Linc mumbles.

I groan, my cheek resting on his strong, warm chest. "I can't. Our CEO is coming and part of the reason she's coming is to see me."

He grunts his disapproval. I sit up, knowing if I don't force myself out of bed, I'll fall back asleep. Fatigue makes my head swim.

"Hang out here with Karma while I'm gone. We can go out tonight and you can meet Genevieve."

His sexy, lazy smile makes me want to curl back up to him, just for five more minutes.

"The famous Genevieve? The one who hordes office supplies and requires Starbucks in the morning and the afternoon?"

I'm touched he remembers. We talked a lot about our friends at the cabin, and he told me about every one of his teammates.

"That's her."

His smile fades slightly. "I wish I could, babe, but I'm flying out early this afternoon."

"Oh. Sure, I understand."

"Hey." He reaches for my hand. "It's not what you're thinking. I didn't just come here for a night of sex. I meant everything I said."

I nod, embarrassed by the tears welling in my

eyes. It's not that I don't believe him; it's that I *just* got him back. And now he's leaving again.

"Let me show you where I'm going." He reaches for his phone on the bedside table and even though I'm bummed he's leaving, I don't miss the opportunity to admire his body.

His muscles are perfectly ridged, his golden skin smooth other than some dark chest hair. He looks more like an artist's take on the perfect man than a real one.

His fingers fly over his phone screen and then he passes it to me. "Scroll through those photos."

The first one is of a sprawling log and stone home that looks straight out of a luxury home magazine. It has two stories, floor-to-ceiling windows and there's a mountain range in the distance. Other photos show a four-stall garage, two separate log buildings and an outdoor space with an in-ground pool and a massive gazebo.

"It's beautiful," I say when I reach the end of the photos.

"I'm glad you think so. Because it's ours."

His gaze is locked on mine, his eyes bright with excitement. It takes me a couple of seconds to find the words to respond. Even then, I can only come up with one.

"*Ours?*"

"I bought it for us. It's outside Jackson Hole, Wyoming. Remember how we talked about our dreams? Yours was to open an animal rescue for cats and dogs and mine was to own a ranch. We can do both of those. Together. I'm going to Jackson Hole today to meet with a builder about converting one of the outbuildings into a space for cats and dogs. We'll add heating and cooling and plumbing so we can give them baths out there."

I just gape at him, words escaping me.

"We've got forty acres. Plenty of room for anything we want."

"Linc...I'm...stunned."

His smile slides away. "Is it a good stunned?"

"I don't know. I'm overwhelmed."

The light fades from his eyes and an ache forms in my chest. I crushed his excitement. I take one of his hands in both of mine.

"Look, I just need some time to process this. Until last night, I didn't even know if you wanted anything with me. And now you tell me you bought a ranch in Wyoming?"

"I thought you'd love it. You don't have to think about money ever again because I saved a lot and invested well. I'm renaming the ranch *Shining Light* because that's what you are to me."

I don't have a choice about it—I cry. I never imagined anyone would do something like this for me. Feel so deeply for me. And I feel just as deeply for him.

I wipe tears from my cheeks and smile at him. "You are the worst communicator ever. I still adore you, though."

"I wanted to surprise you."

I laugh a single note. "This is definitely a surprise."

He sighs heavily. "You're not happy."

"No, Linc. It's not that." I squeeze his hand. "My last boyfriend wanted to split the check when we went to dinner. No one has ever done anything remotely close to this for me. I *am* happy. I'm just also shocked."

He cups one of my cheeks in his hand. "When I was back on the road with my team, I kept wishing I was back at the cabin with you. I want us to have a life where we can wake up every day and do what we love. Cook. Dance. Read. Take a dozen dogs for a walk. Start a garden. And, since I've already shocked you, I might as well go ahead and add that I've changed my thoughts on having kids. I thought I didn't want kids, but...I called my dad and he was happy to hear from me. He wants to have a relationship with me."

"I'm so happy to hear that." My voice is thick with emotion.

"It's not just that, it's also...I hadn't met anyone I wanted any of this with until you. A home and a life and a family. It would be really fucking ironic if I finally found you and you don't feel the same way."

A fresh round of tears floods from my eyes. "Of course I feel the same way. I was just so sure there was no way for us to be together."

His lips quirk up in a smile. "After the cabin, there's no way for us *not* to be together, Trin. Not for me. I always thought my purpose was hockey, but now my purpose is you. Us."

I kiss him, my mind still spinning from the news. "And we don't have to move immediately, right? Like that could be our plan for the future? Because I have my work, and you're retiring, so you could move here."

He opens his mouth to speak, then closes it again.

"What?" My heart races as my anxiety starts setting in.

"I mean...we'll need to talk about things, but I was hoping we could move there soon."

We aren't even engaged. Twenty-four hours ago, I didn't even know he wanted to be with me. And now he's asking me to give up everything I know to start a new life with him.

I've never been late for work in my life, and no matter how much I want to be here having this conversation with him, I can't be late on the day our CEO is coming.

"I'm so sorry, but I have to take a quick shower and get to work. Can we talk later?"

"Yeah, of course."

"When will I see you again?"

He considers. "I'll be at the ranch for a few days getting work plans figured out. Then I have to go back to Minneapolis and get my house there listed and hire movers."

I sigh softly. "So not for a while."

"Yeah. You want to take advantage of me one more time before you go?"

I respond by straddling him, my knees on the bed as I look down at him. Our gazes lock and he slides his hands up the backs of my thighs, over my ass. He sinks his hands into my hips.

It's only been a few hours, but my body still

aches for him. Even though we have a lot to talk about, we only have a few more minutes together, and this is how I want to spend them.

KATE RYKER IS BEAUTIFUL. HER BLOND HAIR COMES to her shoulders and her blue eyes have just a hint of crow's-feet when she smiles, which makes her look both pretty and wise. Her smile is flawless and warm, her body lean with curves in all the right places.

"How are you, Trinity?"

We just finished an Allura group meeting, and now I'm alone in Gloria's office with her and Kate. I can tell Kate isn't just perfunctorily asking how I am; she genuinely cares.

"I think I'm doing pretty well overall. I've given up on expecting things to be the way they were before. It'll never be the same, and that's okay."

"Some experiences change us."

I smile, thinking of Linc blowing me a kiss as I was walking out of my bedroom earlier. He was planning to get a couple more hours of sleep, and it was difficult to make myself leave him.

"That's very true. And sometimes people change us, too," I say.

Kate and Gloria exchange a knowing smile.

"You mean the hockey player?" Gloria asks. "Lincoln?"

"He flew in last night and surprised me."

Gloria claps her hands together, her eyes sparkling with happiness. "I'm delighted to hear it."

"That explains the wet hair," Kate says with a laugh.

My cheeks warm. I took a record-setting two-minute shower and caught an Uber to work, applying my makeup on the ride. I didn't have time to do anything but run a comb through my hair.

"He bought a ranch in Wyoming," I blurt. "For us. Because I said my dream was to have an animal rescue one day. I meant, like, in thirty years."

Kate meets my gaze, her expression amused. "And let me guess, he didn't ask you about it beforehand?"

"No! He hasn't communicated about his feelings over the phone *at all*. I was so upset, thinking it was over between us, and then he shows up and says he loves me and we now own a ranch in Wyoming."

"That sounds about right. He's the team captain, right?"

I shrug. "I mean, he was? But he just decided to retire. He dropped that news on me last night, too."

"He's used to being in charge and having people follow his lead. My husband is the same way."

I knew she was married to a retired hockey player—Jason Ryker—but I'd forgotten that he was also once a team captain.

"How does that work for you and your husband? If you don't mind me asking."

"I don't mind at all. Ryke can be...domineering at times. I say it's one of his best and worst traits. When we disagree and he thinks he's right and I think I'm right...well, buckle up." She laughs. "But he has so much more heart than any other man I've ever known. Everything he does is for our family. Our kids think he hung the moon."

Her voice is filled with pride and affection. She shrugs and shakes her head as she continues. "I mean, I kind of agree. I think he's the best. But we've had to work things out before, like any couple. He once surprised me by reserving an Italian villa for a month during the summer, and I had some meetings scheduled then that I couldn't miss. He doesn't always understand why the company is still important to me even though we're well-off financially. But he got over it and took the kids on a friend's boat for the few days I had to be gone, and it ended up being a wonderful trip. Now he *asks* me before he schedules trips."

I nod. "I love my work here. Getting to help people feel beautiful and confident isn't just a job to me. It's a calling."

"I love hearing that. You're a big part of Allura's success, Trinity. And if your heart tells you to move to Wyoming, there will still be a role for you here if you want it."

I warm inside, smiling as big as my cheeks will allow. "I wouldn't have asked you for that, but it would mean a lot to me to not have to leave completely."

"I'm thrilled for you. You didn't just survive the plane crash—you came out of it stronger. And in love."

I picture Linc sitting across the table from me at the cabin, elbows on the table. His warm gaze on mine. He was a lifeline to me then. A port in a storm of uncertainty and fear. And he still is.

"He loves me exactly as I am, and I want to love him back the same way. Surprise ranch purchase and all."

Kate stands from her seat. "He's a keeper. They're stubborn and sometimes impulsive, but life with a hockey player is never dull. I wish you all the happiness in the world."

I'm still nervous as hell, but it feels real now. With her words of support, what felt overwhelming and impossible this morning now feels like it's truly happening.

I guess I need to buy some cowboy boots.

twenty-six

ONE MONTH LATER

LINCOLN

"Are you sure about this?" My dad gives me a skeptical look as he takes off his straw hat and wipes sweat from his brow. "This is a lot of lettuce for two people."

"I invited my whole team to come visit as soon as their season ends. And their wives and kids."

He arches his brows. "Okay then. You should have some nice salads from this garden."

"There's also a garden co-op in Jackson Hole. I can donate anything we won't be able to use."

Satisfied, he returns to work. He and my stepmom, Pam, came to the ranch for the first time to visit a few days ago. I planned to stop the projects I had in progress and take them sightseeing and out to some of the many great restaurants in the area, but they both insisted they wanted to help me with the ranch.

"Dinner will be ready in fifteen minutes," Pam says, getting up from the spot where she's kneeling on the ground, working the soil with a hand tool. "I'd better get cleaned up."

She's been making dinner every night, and it's the first time in ages I've had home-cooked meals. Tonight we're having beef stew and garlic bread, and after working on tilling the new garden plot all afternoon, I'm so fucking hungry I could chew on one of my hands.

"You should go get a shower," my dad says. "You don't want to be a mess when your girl gets here."

I glance at my watch, which has dirt caked around the band. "Oh, shit. I didn't realize it was so late."

"We're going to wait until she gets here to have dinner."

I stand up and brush dirt off my clothes.

Trinity's finally on her way here. The past month has passed slowly, other than the long weekend I spent with her in Chicago two weeks ago.

We talked a lot and shopped for engagement rings. I'm more sure than ever about us, but I'm nervous about her seeing the ranch.

The setting couldn't be more beautiful, with mountains in the distance and a small lake surrounded by woods. The view from every window is spectacular.

The interior of the main lodge is under renovation, though, and it's currently a mess. There's drywall dust everywhere and plastic sheeting up to keep the dust from covering every surface in the house.

Dad, Pam and I are all staying in the two-bedroom guesthouse for now. It has a kitchen and two bathrooms, so it meets our needs. It's being renovated after the main house. Trinity's been helping choose finishes for everything over FaceTime.

The bathroom I use in the guesthouse has forest-green tile and wallpaper with a border that has cowboy hats all over it. It's still stuck in the year 1991, which is when the lodge and guesthouse were built by a Hollywood producer. He never spent much time here, so the place was frozen in time when I bought it.

It has great potential, though. When I looked at the property for the first time, it reminded me of my relationship with Trin. At first, we saw the green tile and wallpaper in each other. All the red flags and none of the green.

Our time together brought us past that superficial facade. We got to know and appreciate each other on a deeper level. I saw her push back against the anxiety that wanted to put her in a stranglehold. She accepted me as I was, even though I was neurotic about sex because of my own hang-ups.

We saw the best and the worst in each other over our months together. No one has ever known me like she does. The thought of us having a family doesn't scare me in the least. I'd like to take our future kids to Alaska someday and show them the cabin where their parents fell in love.

After I finish shaving and showering, I go out to the kitchen, where my dad is scrubbing his hands at the sink.

"Pam's taking a quick shower. She's nervous about meeting Trinity."

I furrow my brow. "She shouldn't be. Trin's easy to get along with."

"I know, it's just...Pam worries she'll say or do the wrong thing. That's just how she is. She's been hoping we could have a relationship for a long time now."

Even though my dad has told me to leave the past behind and move forward, it's hard to forgive myself for not reaching out to him sooner. If I hadn't survived the crash, he never would have known I found out the truth about my mom deliberately keeping us apart.

"I'm just glad you guys are here."

He smiles. "We are, too. And we're really looking forward to Thanksgiving."

Trin and I offered to host Dad, Pam and all the extended family for Thanksgiving this year. We'll have all the remodeling done by then. Dalton and Trinity's mom will be here, too.

I never cared about holidays before. They were just another day but with turkey for dinner. Alaska changed my thinking on that, though. I want to be a better son, uncle, brother and friend.

The beep that signifies a car at the ranch's front gate sounds and my heart kicks up speed. It has to be Trin. I push the button to open the gate, hoping she sees the new bronze "Shining Light Ranch" plate I had installed at the entrance.

She drove here so she could bring everything from her apartment. She sold all her furniture and only brought what she could fit in her car. I offered to come pick her up in my new truck, but she wanted to stop in Des Moines to have dinner with a friend from college last night.

"Pam, Trinity's here!" Dad calls.

Pam comes rushing from the bedroom they're staying in, running a hand over her short, dark hair. She gives me a quick, excited smile.

"You guys are gonna love her," I say.

We all walk out to the lodge's front entrance, where Trin pulls in and parks. A dark SUV driven by Gideon pulls in behind her. He gives me a wave, turns around and drives back out the gate.

I paid him to follow her here just in case that creep Ronan is still stalking her. Now that she's here, where we have a tight security system and perimeter alarms, he shouldn't be able to get to her. And if he did, he'd have to go through me first.

As soon as Trin steps out of the car, our eyes lock and she runs toward me.

She's more beautiful than ever, wearing jeans, a Mammoths hoodie and tennis shoes, her hair up in a ponytail. I sweep her off her feet in a hug, closing my eyes and inhaling the familiar scent of her soap and light floral perfume.

I keep our kiss quick and PG-rated, even though I want to carry her to the nearest bedroom and do a hell of a lot more.

When I set her feet back on the ground, she smiles at my dad and Pam.

"Hi, I'm Trinity. You must be Tim and Pam."

They both hug her, tears shining in Pam's eyes. I had no idea my stepmom cared for me as much as she did until this visit. Even though she'd never met me, she never gave up hope for my dad and I to mend our relationship.

"I'll unpack your car tomorrow," I say. "Let's just catch up tonight."

"Pam and I are staying at a bed-and-breakfast in Jackson Hole tonight," Dad announces. "We'll be heading there after dinner."

"You don't need to do that," Trinity says. "Stay here. The guesthouse has two bedrooms."

Pam shakes her head. "We want to see more of Jackson Hole. We'll be back tomorrow evening."

I exchange a look with my dad, who winks at me. I guess no one's going to say out loud that they're leaving us alone so we can have all the loud, crazy sex we want tonight.

Which will be a lot. Trin and I have only had a total of four nights together since the first time we had sex. Phone sex doesn't even compare. Her legs and hips will be sore tomorrow after all the positions I've been fantasizing about.

"This place is gorgeous," she says, taking my hand as we walk to the guesthouse.

"You like it?"

She grins. "Linc, I *love* it. The photos don't do it justice."

We spend an hour laughing and talking over dinner, and then I show her around the main lodge. She squeezes my hand with excitement as we move from room to room.

"This is our bedroom."

Her eyes widen as she takes in the mountain view. The room is on the main level and the builders are working on a private patio with French doors. We're combining this room with another bedroom to make a massive primary suite with two walk-in closets, a laundry area and the bathroom of Trin's dreams.

We're having the same style of tub the cabin

has, and I know we'll spend many an evening in it together.

"It's incredible." She kisses me. "I'm so excited."

Back out in the main living area, I gesture at the partially built staircase. "Can't take you upstairs, unfortunately. It should be done in a week or so."

We're replacing a plain staircase with an open, curved one. By the time we're finished with this remodel, the interior of the lodge will be brand new. We'll have seven bedrooms, five bathrooms, a game room, a home theater and an office for Trin.

"I couldn't love it more," she says to me as we finish the tour in the garage. "It's a dream come true. The pantry is the size of the living room in my apartment."

My dad waves from a few feet away. "We'll see you kids tomorrow."

Trin and I pause to hug both of them. She makes plans with Pam for us to meet them in Jackson Hole tomorrow for some shopping and dinner out. Pam looks like she's about to burst with excitement.

"We love you guys," she says on their way out.

"Love you, too," I say.

Trin squeezes my hand as we watch them drive away. She looks up at me.

"They're so great, Linc. I really like them."

"Me too." I tug her ponytail gently. "You look so damn good. I've missed you."

She laughs. "In my hoodie and jeans?"

"You'd look good in anything."

"Well..." she backs up a few steps, giving me a playful look. "I might have something lacy on underneath the hoodie."

I walk toward her. "Yeah? I might need to verify that."

I take her hand and pull her to me, kissing her. She melts against me, moaning as I kiss her deeper.

"Back to the guesthouse," I murmur against her lips. "You'll get drywall dust in your ass crack if we take our clothes off here."

She laughs and cups my cheeks, wrinkling her nose. "I'll pass on that."

I pick her up and walk toward the door, her legs encircling my waist. "To the guesthouse, then. Just like old times."

Her gaze softens. "Are you going to make me fall in love with you all over again?"

I grin at her. "Damned if I'm not gonna try, gorgeous."

epilogue

FIVE MONTHS LATER

TRINITY

IF SOMEONE HAD TOLD ME A BILLIONAIRE TECH executive would one day officiate my wedding to one of my brother's teammates in a remote Alaska cabin, I would have laughed.

But here we are.

When Linc proposed to me three months ago, we both knew immediately we wanted to get married at the cabin where we fell in love. Skyler was thrilled with the idea and honored when we asked him to officiate.

We never thought our friends and family would set foot inside this cabin, and it was interesting to see their reactions when they first walked in about an hour ago. My brother looked from the bathtub to Lincoln. Then back to the tub, to Lincoln again, his eyes narrowed.

Dalton has heard us talk about taking baths here, and he didn't seem pleased when he saw that the cabin is one wide-open room where privacy isn't an option.

He's good with us being together—he's even Linc's best man in the wedding--but he still goes into big brother mode on occasion.

"Without further ado, we are gathered here today to see Lincoln and Trinity pledge their lifetime love and commitment to each other," Skyler says.

We fast-tracked our wedding plans so some of Linc's teammates could be here before their preseason starts. Dane Foster, Aaron Parker and Archer Holt are his groomsmen and Aiden Rogers is a guest. Aaron, Aiden and Archer's wives even came. All three women jumped right into action when they arrived, helping Skyler's assistants get the floral arrangements set up after they were delivered by snowmobile.

We told Skyler all we wanted was a simple wedding in the cabin and to spend our wedding night alone here. But he insisted on hiring an event planner, who had a heated outdoor tent put up outside the cabin. There's a wood floor beneath the tent and a long table set with a white tablecloth and elaborate floral centerpieces.

I realized Skyler was right when I saw the portable bathrooms and a separate tent where my bridesmaids and I got ready for the wedding. That would have been harder with just the cabin and the outhouse.

"We all know theirs was an unconventional courtship," Skyler says, drawing laughs from everyone. "What started as survival blossomed into something beautiful. When I recently stayed with Lincoln and Trinity at their ranch for a few days, Lincoln shared with me that his bride's resilience is one of his favorite things about her. And resilience is a cornerstone of any good marriage."

Linc's gaze is locked onto mine, his hands holding mine. My wedding dress is a simple, off-white, off-the-shoulder gown with long sleeves, pearls dotted over the lace fabric that makes up the sleeves. My hair is down in waves, a delicate beaded tiara atop my head.

I was fortunate to have several cosmetics experts to apply my makeup. Genevieve is my maid of honor and Gloria and Kate are both guests. Three of my close friends from college are my bridesmaids.

Lincoln squeezes my hands gently, taking a deep breath as he starts reciting his vows.

"Trin, we didn't get off on the best foot. You called me a few names and I...*might* have tried to make all the decisions about our survival without asking your opinion. But I've never known anyone who has your strength. You walked miles and miles in the bitter cold with a sprained ankle and you didn't complain. You showed patience with me when I didn't always deserve it. The sun was only out for a few hours a day when we were here, but your smile became my sun. My life is infinitely better with you by my side." His voice trembles with emotion and he pauses to compose himself, Dalton setting a hand on his shoulder. "The worst thing that's ever happened to me is the plane crash, but it led to the best thing that's ever happened to me. You. I promise to love you and be faithful to you for the rest of my life, in good times and in bad. You've made me a better man. I promise to listen, comfort you when you're down, take care of you when you're sick and continue pretending I don't notice when you sneak extra dogs into the house."

There's more laughter and my cheeks warm. I really thought I was slipping that by him. We have thirteen dogs who live in our outdoor kennel building, and some of them have always been outdoor-only dogs. But my heart can't resist bringing them inside sometimes for snuggles and extra treats.

"Being your husband will be the greatest privilege of my life. I promise to earn it every day, with everything I am."

He wipes the corner of one eye and I squeeze his hands, impressed he memorized all that. My vows are shorter and I read them from the paper Genevieve passes me.

"Lincoln, you're my person. My best friend and my partner in all things. If I could make myself a perfect man, he still wouldn't measure up to you." I stop to take a breath and fight back the tears pooling in my eyes. "You make me laugh and you take care of me in every way, both big and small. I promise to love you through every storm that comes our way. To always look to you first and never let anyone else inside the sacred walls of our marriage. I love you with my whole heart, today and forever."

I didn't want to cry, but I can't help it. I'm overcome with emotion. We're back in the cabin where we first held on to each other and never let go. His dad and stepmom and my mom are here. Even his sister Alexandra made the trip all the way from North Carolina, where she lives with her family.

Alexandra and her husband Mike have seven-year-old twins, a boy and a girl named Chase and Charlotte. Linc and I got to have the kids at the ranch for two weeks over the summer, and we had a blast with them. We have a horse at the ranch, Gordie, and the kids couldn't get enough of riding him, playing with our dogs and hiking through the woods with us.

When Skyler tells Linc he can kiss his bride, I'm officially an aunt. And I hope to soon become a mother, too. We plan to start trying for our first child after Christmas.

I work two days a week as a remote consultant for Allura, and I love it. The rest of the time, Linc and I keep busy with our home and our animals. We cook dinner together every night. Soon we'll be tuning in to every hockey game the Mammoths play in our home theater.

Linc hopes to get into coaching at some point.

He doesn't care if it's hockey or another sport. He just wants to help kids connect with sports the way he did when he was young.

Our guests congratulate us and slowly flow out to the tent for the reception. Linc and I find ourselves alone in the cabin, standing in the center of it with his arms around my waist and mine around his shoulders.

"I feel like we should be making some beans and rice on the hot plate," he cracks. "Maybe getting ready to play some Boggle."

"We get to stay here tonight. We're definitely playing Boggle before we consummate this marriage."

His grin is sexy. "Strip Boggle."

I laugh. "You'll be naked before me, guaranteed."

"We'll see. I believe I'm the one with the 217–195 Boggle record, big talker."

"Yes, but I've been practicing on my phone."

He kisses me, his eyes sparkling with happiness. "Can't we just let everyone else have the reception while we stay here?"

"It's just a few hours and then we'll be alone."

With a reluctant sigh, he gives in, then kisses me

again. I smile up at him, happiness radiating warmly through me.

"How you liking marriage so far, Mrs. Rowe?"

"It's everything I ever hoped for."

"Just wait 'til tonight."

He winks and leads me toward the door. I glance back at the cabin, my gaze wandering over the full-size bed we shared, the record player and the simple kitchen. Then I turn and walk through the door with my husband, knowing a beautiful future lies ahead of us.

want more?

The next book in the Minnesota Mammoths series is Drawn to You.

also by brenda rothert

CHICAGO BLAZE SERIES

Book 1 - Anton

Book 2 - Luca

Book 3 - Victor

Book 4 - Knox

Book 5 - Alexei

Book 6 - Easy

Book 7 - Jonah

Book 8 - Kit

Book 9 - Olivier

COLORADO COYOTES SERIES

Book 1 - The Donor

Book 2 - The Opponent

Book 3 - The Proposal

Book 4 - The Imposter

Book 5 - The Face-Off

SIN CITY SAINTS SERIES

Book 1 - Maverick

Book 2 - Pike

Book 3 - Pax

St. Lous Mavericks series

Book 1 - Hard Fall

Book 2 - Hard Limit

Book 3 - Hard Pass

Book 4 - Hard Luck

Book 5 - Hard Hit

Fire on Ice Series

Book 1 - Bound

Book 2 - Captive

Book 3 - Edge

Book 4 - Drive

Book 5 - Release

On the Line Series

Book 1 - Killian

Book 2 - Bennett

Lockhart Brothers Series

Book 1 - Deep Down

Book 2 - In Deep

Book 3 - Drawn Deeper

Book 4 - Hidden Depth

Filthy Series

Book 1 - Dirty Work

Book 2 - Dirty Secret

Book 3 - Dirty Defiance

Standalones

Come Closer

Buried

Sweet Sixteen

His

Alpha Mail

Healing Touch

Barely Breathing

Exiled

Unspoken

about the author

Brenda Rothert lives in Central Illinois with her husband, children and two dogs. She loves to hear from readers through her website or her Facebook Group, Rothert's Readers.

www.ingramcontent.com/pod-product-compliance
Lightning Source LLC
Chambersburg PA
CBHW011320310726

48973CB00011B/2992